MW01075589

A NOVEL BASED ON THE LIFE OF
ANGELO DUNDEE

A BOXING TRAINER'S
JOURNEY

Jonathan Brown

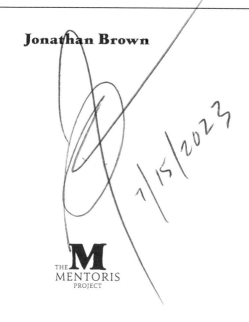

THE
M
MENTORIS
PROJECT

Barbera Foundation, Inc.
P.O. Box 1019
Temple City, CA 91780

Copyright © 2018 Barbera Foundation, Inc.
Cover photo: Trinity Mirror / Mirrorpix / Alamy Stock Photo
Cover design: Suzanne Turpin

More information at www.mentorisproject.org

ISBN: 978-1-947431-20-1

Library of Congress Control Number: 2018957768

The Mentoris Project is a series of novels and biographies about the lives of great men and women who have changed history through their contributions as scientists, inventors, explorers, thinkers, and creators. The Barbera Foundation sponsors this series in the hope that, like a mentor, each book will inspire the reader to discover how she or he can make a positive contribution to society.

Contents

Foreword

First and foremost, Mentor was a person. We tend to think of the word *mentor* as a noun (a mentor) or a verb (to mentor), but there is a very human dimension embedded in the term. Mentor appears in Homer's *Odyssey* as the old friend entrusted to care for Odysseus's household and his son Telemachus during the Trojan War. When years pass and Telemachus sets out to search for his missing father, the goddess Athena assumes the form of Mentor to accompany him. The human being welcomes a human form for counsel. From its very origins, becoming a mentor is a transcendent act; it carries with it something of the holy.

The Mentoris Project sets out on an Athena-like mission: We hope the books that form this series will be an inspiration to all those who are seekers, to those of the twenty-first century who are on their own odysseys, trying to find enduring principles that will guide them to a spiritual home. The stories that comprise the series are all deeply human. These books dramatize the lives of great men and women whose stories bridge the ancient and the modern, taking many forms, just as Athena did, but always holding up a light for those living today.

Whether in novel form or traditional biography, these books plumb the individual characters of our heroes' journeys.

The power of storytelling has always been to envelop the reader in a vivid and continuous dream, and to forge a link with the subject. Our goal is for that link to guide the reader home with a new inspiration.

What is a mentor? A guide, a moral compass, an inspiration. A friend who points you toward true north. We hope that the Mentoris Project will become that friend, and it will help us all transcend our daily lives with something that can only be called holy.

—Robert J. Barbera, President, Barbera Foundation
—Ken LaZebnik, Founding Editor, The Mentoris Project

Prologue

The morning of November 5, 1994, Angelo Dundee was lying back in the oversized king bed in his MGM Grand Hotel room. As he gazed at the plain yellow ceiling, which was a welcome contrast to the busy pattern of the two-tone brown wall-to-wall carpet, he let his mind drift. As one of the world's top professional boxing trainers, the road behind him was lengthy—he'd worked with fighters of every weight class and of several ethnicities. The road's surface was made of canvas and littered with boxing gloves, heavy bags, blood, and hand wraps. Not many chose to travel this route, but it was a path Angelo regarded with fondness.

With a slow turn of his head, he looked to the journey ahead, his future career path. The distance seemed much shorter. He was seventy-three. Would he know when it was time to turn his back to the ring ropes and descend the stairs for the last time? He'd seen far too many boxers, and trainers too for that matter, chase "just one more fight" only to have it end badly. Angelo had no desire to join that statistic.

He sat up and let the thoughts roll off him like an outgoing tide. It was the morning of one of the biggest fights of his career and Angelo needed to be razor sharp. Not only were his days as a trainer numbered, but his fighter and good friend "Big George" Foreman would be stepping into the ring that very evening, perhaps for his final time.

After a ten-year layoff, George had been putting together an impressive comeback. What began as a means for him to raise money for his church led him to Angelo and ultimately a shot at the heavyweight title. Angelo not only respected George and his mission, but working with him had strengthened Angelo's faith in God, men, and boxing.

Angelo did his usual morning light callisthenic stretches—something recently adopted at the gentle request of his doctor—then took a shower. He ate breakfast alone in his room and went over all possible scenarios of George's upcoming fight with the hard-hitting Michael Moorer. It was a good matchup for George, but it would be no cakewalk.

After finishing his eggs, he took his coffee and sat in the room's cozy seating area and thought about his time with George. He'd come to truly love the gentle giant. George had a smile for everyone he met and a wonderful self-deprecating humor. He'd completely changed and dispatched the angry man he'd been in his youth. As far as training, Angelo couldn't have asked for a more symbiotic working relationship. George did things his way and his way was right for George. And Angelo, being a don't-fix-what-ain't-broke type of trainer, had the smoothest of rides training George.

The hours passed quickly and now it was fight night. Both

Big George, the forty-five-year-old fan-favorite, and Angelo, the aging trainer, were more than ready. If George beat Michael Moorer, he'd be the oldest heavyweight to hold the title.

The bell rang. Moorer seemed to have George's number from the get-go. He was ahead on the scorecards. Angelo instructed George to be patient and fight *his* fight, and that's exactly what George had been doing. But the rounds were adding up. An uneasy feeling came to Angelo's stomach. He didn't want his guy to lose, but more importantly, he didn't want Geroge, his fighter and friend, to get hurt.

The bell sounded for the tenth round. By the middle of the round, George launched his big bear paw of a right hand straight down the pipe.

A loud pop sounded and was heard around the world . . . and then the planet stopped rotating on its axis.

Chapter One

BOXING, FAMILY, AND UNCLE SAM

Angelo Dundee was born Angelo Mirena on August 30, 1921. The Mirenas enjoyed a simple life in South Philadelphia in the early 1920s. It was a time when women wore dresses that flowed below the knee, and men wore hats: bowlers, fedoras, pork pies. The entire city seemed to be made of brick and concrete. Model Ts, Model As, and Chryslers could be seen rolling down South Philly's wide streets.

Ten-year-old Angelo was about to explode with excitement. No, it wasn't his birthday, or Christmas. It was Sunday, the day his mother laid out her famous feast. His mouth had been watering all day. He looked forward to this all week, every week, as did his siblings.

When Angelo's mother sent him on an errand before dinner, he did his best not to dawdle, as was his usual custom. The young boy was incredibly social and he was ready for conversation with just about anybody. But today he kept his pleasantries short and was nearing home when he literally bumped into Freddie, the neighborhood bully. Any kid with sense avoided Freddie.

Some of Angelo's friends were there with him, but they wouldn't help. Fear had paralyzed them—nobody wanted to attract a bully's attention, especially one as cruel as Freddie. There was no reasoning with the brutish kid; Angelo had seen others try. Fighting was not Angelo's strongest suit—that was his brothers' forte. Now, he realized he was going to have to defend himself alone.

Angelo put his hands up like he'd seen his siblings do while play-boxing at home. Freddie moved in slowly with a huge grin of overconfidence spreading across his big block head. Angelo was forced to look up, since Freddie had nearly six inches on him, and easily weighed twenty-five pounds more than he did. Angelo was pudgy, but Freddie actually had muscles. The smaller boy tried hard not to stare at his big arms—too scary.

Freddie moved forward with his hands casually at his sides.

"Time to pay the price, fat boy."

Angelo hated being called that. The circle of friends closed around the two boys. Angelo decided to take the first swing. He might score one of those "lucky punches" he'd heard about so many times. He lunged forward with a big haymaker, wanting to take Freddie's block off. Freddie saw it coming as if he'd received a telegram last week. In an instant Angelo knew he'd overcommitted. He wondered if his friends were thinking *poor kid* as Freddie stepped aside and shoved him hard in the back.

Pain shot through Angelo's kneecap as he hit the ground. He tried to get to his feet but Freddie's full weight collapsed on top of him. It felt like a big lead anvil pushing into his chest. Angelo immediately covered his head with his plump arms as Freddie dropped a barrage of punches down on him.

Terrified, Angelo held his own—sort of. His knee hurt but he managed to take all of the blows to the arms. Surely a grownup would happen by soon. *Hang in there*, he told himself.

Then, a fist finally slipped through the defense right to Angelo's nose. It stung. His eyes watered but he forced himself not to cry. His brothers wouldn't respect that. Now more than ever, he wished he could fight like them.

"You want some more, fat boy?" Freddie laughed.

Mrs. Cosco, their neighbor, suddenly bustled up and swatted Freddie over the head with a newspaper.

Swat! "Stop this, Frederico." *Swat!* "I'm gonna tell your momma." *Swat!* "Now, go home!"

Freddie got off his victim and strolled down the street, laughing all the way.

Angelo looked up gratefully. "Thanks, Mrs. Cosco."

"It's okay. Why are you out here? Why aren't you at home? Go eat your momma's food. Be a good boy."

"Yes, Mrs. Cosco."

She turned to the friends standing by. "You boys, why didn't you stop Frederico?" She shook her paper at them, and they cringed away. "You have to stick up for each other. Now, go."

"Yes, Mrs. Cosco." They responded as a chorus, their eyes downcast.

Angelo thanked the kind lady a second time, then checked his nose. Yup, it was bleeding. Darn it. He hobbled back home as fast as his aching knee would allow, stopping every few feet to rub it.

As he walked through the door at home, his mother ran to him.

"What happened? Have you been fighting?"

Held tightly in his mother's arms, he allowed the tears to come.

"There, there, Angie. Why you fighting? You a good boy."

He sobbed a little more before pulling away from his mother. Older brother Jimmy was standing with legs wide beside the kitchen sink. His fists clenched and unclenched at his sides.

"Who was it?"

"It was Fre-Freddie," Angelo stammered.

"De Luca?"

"Yeah, Jimmy."

"How long 'til dinner, Ma?" Jimmy asked.

"Jimmy, don't you go—"

"How long, Ma?"

"*Quindici minuti.*" Fifteen minutes.

Jimmy bolted out the door. Angelo looked at his mother, who shook her head, then sprinted out the door after Jimmy.

A few blocks away, parked outside Mr. Johnson's gray brick barbershop, was a black Chrysler B70. Freddie De Luca leaned against the car, bragging to his friends.

"I was pounding on that fat Mirena kid and—"

The other kids stopped laughing as they saw Jimmy approach from behind.

"Hey, Freddie, why don't ya pound on *this* Mirena kid?"

Freddie took flight but Jimmy was too quick. Rounding the corner, Angelo watched his big brother do to Freddie what Freddie had done to him. He felt conflicted—he was delighting in seeing the bully get his due but felt guilty that someone other than himself had to fight his battle. Shame washed over him. A wave of nausea followed as he heard Freddie beg for mercy. Angelo nearly vomited.

Finally, the beating was over. Freddie lay in a heap of tears. Jimmy put an arm around Angelo's shoulders and steered him toward home.

"You feel bad, don't you, Ang? I know you, you're a sensitive kid."

"I don't know how I feel, Jimmy."

"Look, he's older and bigger than you. I'm older and bigger than him. Sometimes it just works that way in life. There's always somebody bigger and tougher than somebody else. Remember that, Angelo."

"Okay, Jimmy."

"Now then, whaddya gonna do about it?"

"I want to learn to fight. Ya know, so nobody messes with me."

"That's the spirit. Me and your brother Frankie, we gonna take you down to the Mason Hall AC Gym and teach you how to box. But ya can't tell Pop, okay?"

Angelo nodded his agreement.

"Let's go eat. We gotta run because if we're late, Pop will beat us worse than anything you saw today. What's he always say?"

Angelo loved it when his brothers asked him to do his Pop impersonation.

"Boys, yo mamma, she work hard to make-a da meal. Show her some respect and be on time for it, will ya?"

Angelo nailed it, voice and mannerisms. Jimmy laughed and mussed his little brother's hair.

"Let's go. Hustle up now."

The entire run home, Angelo trailed behind Jimmy with a big grin on his face. Gosh, he loved his brothers almost as much as he loved the homemade pasta he was about to wolf down.

⌇

Angelo's brothers did exactly as promised and taught their little brother the basics of boxing. Angelo loved everything about the gym, especially the sounds of gloves striking bags and the skipping ropes whistling through the air as they barely grazed the gym floor. He even loved the sweaty smell of the joint. He observed everything, taking it in like a student in a master class.

The more he went to the place, the more he physically changed. He began to lose excess weight and develop muscles. By age fifteen, he was lean and toned. It was a shame that boxing didn't add height to a fellow, but in the parlance of South Philly, "them's the breaks."

One Saturday afternoon while leaving the gym, he bumped into Freddie. He knew he'd face down his former tormentor someday. South Philly was a small town after all, but he wasn't sure how it would play out.

They were the only two people in the alley between Morris and Main. Both stopped in their tracks. Angelo was nervous, but not like the old days. He noticed that Freddie didn't seem quite so ominous as he had years before. He'd developed a potbelly and he sort of dragged his feet when he walked. Angelo regarded Freddie's hands and realized he was sizing up his opponent the way a bona fide boxer would. As his body filled with confidence, he noticed Freddie becoming apprehensive.

"Hiya, Ang."

Freddie cast his eyes to the street and shuffled past, maintaining a wide berth. Angelo walked home with a grin on his face and a little puffiness to his chest. A foe had been vanquished.

~

It was Angelo's final year of high school. Franklin Delano Roosevelt was the thirty-second president of the United States, Judy Garland's "Over the Rainbow" topped the charts, and Joe Louis was boxing's heavyweight champion of the world.

Angelo began to think about the job market. Part-time jobs were expected in the Mirena family and all seven siblings (Joe, Chris, Mary, Frankie, Jimmy, Angelo, and Josephine) pitched in. At the time, Angelo was playing football and was a decent defensive lineman. His best buddy, Rick, also a D-lineman, gave him a tip on a job at Pat's Steak House.

Through his connections, Rick got Angelo an interview. Pat, the owner, loved the work ethic that the young man brought with him, which Pop Mirena had instilled in each of his children. When it came time to get his first paycheck, Angelo was proud to bring the earnings home to his mother and do his part. In return, if he needed anything, all he had to do was ask his mother and she would get it for him. But Angelo rarely wanted or needed anything.

The only thing he insisted on was his mother's cooking. If anyone thought that the perk of working at a steak house was gorging on a T-bone, Angelo knew nothing about it, nor cared to. On lunch breaks, he told Frankie to hop on his bike and bring his mother's pasta back to Pat's restaurant. He looked forward to it during the first half of his shift, and a full belly of delicious spaghetti carried him through the end of the work day. Nothing else came close to Mom's cooking.

The surname "Dundee" first caught on with Angelo's oldest

brother, Joe. The secret was revealed on the back steps of Pat's. One day on break, Angelo sat eating the pasta that his brother Frankie had brought by via bicycle.

"Angelo, you know why Joe changed his name to Dundee, right?"

"So Pop wouldn't know he's boxing?"

"But do you know why *Dundee*?"

"Jimmy told me that fighter Joey Corrara gave it to him."

"Joey Corrara had nearly three hundred fights. But a big problem is, nobody outside of South Philly knows how to say his name, so he changed it to Johnny Dundee. Our brother Joe was always a big fan of Joey. He's got a mean left hook and a sneaky one at that. Guys just don't see it coming. Anyway, Joe took the name Dundee in honor of his hero, Johnny Dundee."

"So that's why . . . whaddya know? " Angelo said softly.

"How about it? Gonna change your name to Dundee?"

"I don't know about that, Frankie, but I do know this—I'm gonna be in the fight game somehow. Don't get me wrong, I like football well enough, but boxing does something to me. I can't even explain it."

"You're good, but it's tough to be great. Ya know what I mean?"

"I'll figure it out."

Angelo finished off the remains of his dinner.

"Tell Mom it was delicious as usual. I gotta get back to work. Thanks for always doing this, brother. I know it's a pain in the butt."

"You were always a pain in the butt," he laughed.

They hugged briefly before Angelo stepped back into the restaurant. Frankie jumped on his bike, balancing the plate with one hand, and rode away.

~

By this time, Angelo had joined the AC Rio Football team and started at the defensive end position. He was in great shape and had a dynamite tan. Those were the tools that he needed for the one thing more important than boxing—girls! He and a couple other fellows on the team adopted the name "Rio Boys." They weren't so much a gang as just a tight group of lads in hot pursuit of dames.

The Rio Boys had the perfect girl for Angelo. Her name was Becky Russo.

"She's the same age as you and she's a knockout," Rick boasted. "I told her all about you, and guess what? She wants to meet you."

"Come on, you're pulling my leg."

"Nah, it's true, I swear."

"I was there when Rick talked to her," a voice butted in. It was Eddie, the quarterback.

Angelo thought that if this information came from Eddie, it had to be true. Eddie was a good quarterback and a promising leader.

"What happens next?" Angelo asked, surprised at how nervous he was.

"It's all set for tomorrow night. We'll take Eddie's car because she lives about twenty minutes outside of town in a farmhouse. Her parents will be out at a dance so, basically, she's all yours. Tell me you won't chicken out."

"Who, me? Who ya kidding? I've been waiting for something like this for goodness knows how long. What time do we roll?"

"We'll pick you up at Pat's after your shift."

"Should I bring a nice shirt to change into?"

"Ha, I think he's ready, boys," Rick laughed.

Angelo hoped he'd hidden his nervousness from his friends. His legs were shaky as he walked home. The only experiences he had with girls so far were a few make-out sessions, and those he could count on one hand. He'd never had a setup so serious that a girl's parents were out for the night. Man, was he scared! He'd never even met this girl.

He wondered if he should talk to his older brothers about it. *Nah, just be a man*, he told himself. *You can do it.*

He didn't sleep that night, but instead tossed and turned until the sun came up. His emotions vacillated between excitement and terror. During his shift at Pat's, he did his work on automatic pilot. He barely had any words for Frankie as he wolfed down his pasta.

"Sorry, Frankie, I'm just kinda tired is all."

"I know, it sounded like you were in a twelve-round bout in your bed last night. What's eating you?"

"Nothing. I'll be all right."

Frankie scooped up the plate and rode away.

At the end of shift, Angelo took out the garbage, then walked over to Eddie's ride.

"There he is, the man of the hour. Ready to change your life?" Rick teased. He let Angelo hop in the back seat. Rick, Eddie, and three other Rio Boys were already in the car.

"What's with the party, fellas?" Angelo asked.

"We're here for support," Vinnie, the defensive tackle, said.

"And I'm here to take your place when you chicken out, Mirena," Dave, the offensive guard, said with a laugh. They mussed Angelo's hair and playfully roughed him up.

"Watch the hair, I got a date tonight," Angelo pleaded.

"It's not your hair she's interested in, Mirena," Vinnie teased.

"Knock it off, will ya, fellas," Angelo said feebly, before joining in on the laughter.

Twenty minutes later, as promised, they arrived at the end of a long driveway leading to a big dark farmhouse.

"Mirena, it's time to get out of the chariot and go take what's yours," Rick bantered. "We'll wait here for about five minutes just to make sure you're all squared away. After that you're on your own. You got cab fare, right?"

"Sure he does, Rick, he's a high roller. He works at Pat's," Vinnie said, causing laughs.

"I don't know, fellas, it looks awfully dark up there," Angelo said.

"Maybe she'll turn a night light on for ya," Eddie mocked.

Angelo climbed out of the car and headed up the driveway. He pulled his shoulders back and puffed his chest out as far as he could. The Rio Boys would see a confident man marching to his destiny. But in reality, his legs were trembling. He wanted to turn back so bad it hurt.

As he placed his foot on the bottom step of the porch, a light came on and the front door flew open. A large man with a shotgun leveled came barreling out to the edge of the porch.

"*I'm Becky's father and I know the whole thing, Mirena.* Becky told me everything. What kind of boy drives all the way out here to do who-knows-what with a girl he's never met before? *Answer me!*"

"N-n-no, sir, it's not like that. We, we were just going to talk and maybe have a soda or something." Angelo nearly wet his pants. He'd never had a gun pointed at him before.

"*You think I'm a fool, Mirena?*"

"No, no, sir, you seem smart . . . intelligent, even."

"I'm going to count to three and—"

Angelo didn't need to hear any more. He took off running down the driveway. After twenty yards, the shotgun blasted behind him. He ducked and kept pumping his legs. He was thanking God he played football when he reached the car in record time.

The guys were all outside the car, rolling with laughter. Angleo looked at them, stupefied. Slowly it dawned on him that the whole thing was a prank. He's been set up all the way.

"Too bad Coach wasn't here to see how fast you ran, Mirena. He might even make you wide receiver," Vinnie howled.

Becky and the large man came down the driveway, laughing as well. The guys told the truth in between gales of laughter. Becky's "father" was actually her older brother-in-law.

Becky walked up to Angelo.

"I'm sorry about this," she said sweetly. "If it's any consolation, you're not the first guy they've done this to."

She tipped on her toes and kissed him gently on the cheek.

"Well," Angelo said, spreading his arms wide. "It wasn't a total bust. At least I got a kiss on the cheek from a beautiful dame." He took an exaggerated bow.

The laughter went all the way into the following week. When the Rio Boys set up their next victim, Angelo was one of the guys in the back of the car partaking in the laughs.

Two weeks after the prank, the Rio Boys played their rival team, the AC Yellow Jackets. The game was a seesaw battle, neither team holding the lead for long. Near the end of the game, Angelo did a crisscross with the tackle, came up the middle, and put a devastating hit on the quarterback. As Angelo received celebratory pats to the helmet and shoulders, he noticed the quarterback didn't get up.

Running over to investigate, he didn't need a doctor to tell him that he'd broken the boy's leg. Angelo felt horrible. Sure, he wanted to win, but bust a guy's leg? No thanks. The Rio Boys won the game, but it was bittersweet for Angelo.

He found out the name of the hospital where the boy was recovering and went to visit that same evening. He'd asked his mother to make a little extra pasta. When his mother heard the reason, she was only too happy to oblige.

"Hey, Hawkins, your first name is Phil, right?"

"Yeah, you're Mirena. You laid the hit on me."

"Yes, sir. I'm here to apologize and tell you it wasn't intentional. I don't play dirty."

A tear rolled down Phil's face, which he quickly wiped away.

"I guess you know I'm out for the season."

Angelo nodded.

"What's that?" Phil's eyes swept the package in the visitor's hand.

"It's my mother's pasta. It's gonna be better than anything they make around here—double-wrapped in foil so it'll stay hot for a while. I'll put it here by the—"

"The hell you will. Homemade pasta by an Italian? Give it here, man, I'm going to eat that right now."

Angelo handed it over with a big smile. Phil Hawkins dug in. His freckled face grew with an ear-to-ear grin after the first bite. The two boys exchanged some awkward football talk, but when the subject moved to girls, both boys relaxed and even managed to enjoy each other's company.

"That's good. I haven't eaten since before the game. Tell your mom thanks, would ya?"

"Will do."

"You pressured me pretty good all game, Mirena."

17

Angelo didn't know what to say. He just nodded.

"You didn't have to come," he paused. "But I'm glad you did. Not a lot of guys would have. You're all right, Mirena. We're good, you and me."

"Thanks, Phil. You're one hell of a quarterback. Hard to get to."

Angelo got up to leave and stopped at the door.

"I'll say a prayer for your speedy recovery," he said.

"I'm not big on religion but I'll take whatever I can get at this point," he said, forcing a laugh.

"I'll be seein' ya, Phil."

Three weeks later, the Rio Boys were back on the field for the final game. It was no contest. The Rio Boys trounced the Badgers by twenty-two points. On the way to the locker room, Angelo saw Phil Hawkins in the stands with his parents. Angelo walked up the bleachers and met with Phil.

"Good game, Mirena."

"Thanks."

"These are my parents, Mindy and Dean."

They all shook hands.

"That was very nice what you did for our boy," Phil's dad said to Angelo.

"Yes, and I want your mother's pasta recipe. Phillip won't stop talking about it," Phil's mother added.

"She's right here. This is my mother, Philomena, and my father, also."

A pleasant introduction went on for a few minutes before Angelo excused himself. He needed to get to the locker room.

"That's right, you're stinking up the stands, pal," Phil teased.

Later that evening, Pop Mirena told him how proud he was of how he'd handled the situation with Phil Hawkins.

"What you did showed a strong character. You keep it up and you'll make out all right in this world."

The year was 1944 and Angelo, now twenty-three, had fallen in love with dancing, and also with his first dance partner, Rita Carlone. They were dance partners for a year, practicing as often as possible and entering as many contests as they could find. Outwardly, their focus was dancing, but Angelo secretly wanted to spend every waking minute with Rita. He could think of no more innocent excuse to hold on to a beautiful woman. He loved the perfume she wore, and the lemony scent of her thick auburn-colored hair.

Eventually, the couple got together for walks, lunch, or to buy ice cream. After eighteen months, they became engaged. Life was grand until the one thing Angelo feared happened.

"Why so blue?" Rita asked as they sat at their favorite park bench.

Without a word Angelo handed her a government document. Rita looked it over with knitted brows.

"Uncle Sam wants me, honey. I'm joining the fight. After basic training I'll be stationed in London."

Marriage would have to wait. Angelo didn't want to go to war. He'd just gotten engaged, for heaven's sake. He wanted to stay in Philly and build a life with his bride-to-be. But Angelo also believed in the honor of serving his country. Besides, he was no coward, far from it.

As the day of deployment neared, the family gathered for a big send-off dinner. His mother made gnocchi, seeing as they'd had pasta the previous Sunday. Rita and her parents came by. The conversation was surprisingly upbeat. Older brother Jimmy had already joined the war effort and was doing fine—he swore there was nothing to worry about.

After the Carlones went home, Angelo sat down with his father.

"Are you nervous, son?"

"A little, Pop."

"That's okay, that's normal. I'd be worried if you were excited to get over there. I'd think you were *pazzo*," he laughed.

"No. Pop, I'm not crazy. I'm gonna miss you guys. Rita too."

"You'll be all right, son. You're the kinda guy a gal waits for, don't you worry."

"Thanks, Pop."

Because Uncle Sam had tapped him on the shoulder, Angelo answered and dove headlong into army life. Up to this point, he had been working in aircraft maintenance in town, which was how he could afford to take Rita around. But his clerical skills were what the army wanted from him. For the past year he'd taken typing and clerical courses. They were backup, just in case the aircraft maintenance job ever fell through. Angelo didn't kid himself that he'd ever go to college—the family had no money for that. Now it seemed he'd be putting his clerical skills to work for the country.

After two weeks of basic training, he was sent to Leicester-shire, England. The food was foreign and Mom's home cooking seemed far away. It was also a long way from the dance halls of Philly. The weather was cold, wet, and misty. At times he wondered if he'd ever see the sun again.

Life on the base was not bad, and he got along with most of the guys. The locals were friendly to the Americans and seemed happy to have them. One problem at base camp, however, was racism. Angelo had no time for racial bigotry. There seemed to be a natural segregation, which Angelo found odd, considering everybody was fighting on the same side. He felt the base commander should have encouraged some sort mingling or interaction to facilitate team spirit.

"How come you hang out with them coloreds?" a guy named Barrie asked Angelo.

"Why not? They're some good guys."

"Where you from, Mirena?"

"South Philly. Why?"

"I'm from South Carolina and y'all don't know coloreds like we do."

"Keep your voice down," Angelo said, getting off his bunk. "Look, Barrie, I don't care what color a guy is. I either take to a guy or I don't, depending on how he acts."

"I don't see why they need to be on this base. They should have their own base."

Angelo sighed heavily. "I see that you wear a cross around your neck along with your dog tags."

"Yeah, so?"

"As a Christian, you should know that we're all God's children, even black people. Now, would you mind moving aside? It's feeling kinda crowded in here."

Angelo knew the man stared at his back as he left. He was happy Barrie had sense enough not to throw out some kind of cheap line.

Weapons inventory was the next job he was tasked with and he took it seriously and thrived in the position. He completely reworked the filing system and logs. Sergeant Briggs commended him on a job well done, and promised that he'd earn sergeant stripes for the effort. But on the day the promotion list went up,

Angelo found he'd been passed over—he'd remain a Private First Class, or PFC.

The prospect was upsetting. He talked it over with some of the guys and was told "that's Air Corps life." Angelo took it in stride, and went about his business.

A few days later, a care package arrived from his mother. It went a long way to brighten his day. She'd sent salami, capocollo, and pepperoni, as well as pecorino and sharp cheddar cheese. A visit to the base kitchen yielded a few other basic ingredients and he was able to put together a small version of the tastes of home. He gave two soldiers a bite of his food, and they were hooked.

Before Angelo could say "dinner is served," he'd become the barrack chef. His barrack mates couldn't get enough of that South Philly Italian food. In no time, a few of the men converted a potbelly heater into a stove for Angelo's use. Now, letters sent back home always included profuse thanks and ended with a polite, "Ma, please send more."

"Gather 'round, boys," Angelo announced.

The men shuffled around him as if they were parishioners.

"Fellas, I've got an idea to take our cuisine to the next level."

"We're all ears, Mirena. What do you need?" asked Billings, a lanky kid from Arkansas.

"No doubt you've all seen our little rabbit friends running around the camp?"

He got a dozen nods.

"Get me a half dozen rabbits, and I'll cook you a meal like you've never had before."

"Rabbits? I don't know, Mirena. I ain't had no rabbit before." Casey, the big Oregonian, looked skeptical.

"It's 'cause you city slickers don't know good cooking, ain't that right, Curtis?" Scuggs, the red-headed Oklahoman, smiled.

"You better believe it, Mirena. We'll get you them rabbits. Come on, fellas," Curtis said, leading the group outside.

Angelo and six other men stood side by side and watched an area crawling with rabbits.

"On my mark, fellas," Angelo said, adopting a wide firing stance. "Fire!"

All the weaponry exploded at once. Rabbits ran serpentine, zig-zigged, and sprinted in circles. A hail of bullets tore up the gravel and dirt. It sounded like the whole camp was blowing up. Angelo covered an ear with one hand and continued firing his Browning Hi-Power. Each man fired until the weapon clicked empty. Dust and gunpowder swirled around them. As the men lowered weapons, silence fell over the base.

Then a roar of laughter erupted from a group of onlookers.

"Nice job, fellas. You morons didn't hit a single rabbit!"

The shredded ground was empty except for a few torn-up plants. The laughter carried on for minutes. Finally, Angelo moved toward a building on his left.

"Where you off to, Mirena?"

"I gotta go inventory all these darned bullets we wasted," he chuckled. He took an exaggerated bow for the group.

Curtis turned to Casey and said, "Now what are we gonna eat?"

The laughter kept up during Angelo's entire walk to the weapons building.

A few weeks later, Angelo was summoned by his CO to the office. To his surprise, brother Jimmy was standing beside the officer. They hugged so hard that Jimmy begged for air. The two brothers were dismissed and granted an hour to catch up before reporting to a Sergeant Higgins for their next assignment.

"Let's go grab a quick beer," Jimmy said.

"You got it, but I'm paying."

"Like heck you are, you're still a PFC."

"I won't argue that."

Jimmy and Angelo sat down at a quiet table away from the busy section of the bar.

"So what do you think the assignment is?"

"I don't think, I know."

"So give it up, what is it?"

"Some officer is a big fan of Chris."

"Our brother Chris?" Angelo asked incredulously.

"Yup. They know that we're here and that we have a boxing background."

"Boxing background? What the—"

"Didn't you have a boxing match on the ship on the way over here?"

"It was just—"

"And you won, if the rumors is true. Anyway, you popped up on the officer's radar and, as I said, they love Chris and the boxing promotion he's doing."

"Okay, so what's the assignment? Where are you going with this?"

"We're going to be official cornermen for the European Operations Theater—ETO. They think we're experts, all thanks to Chris Dundee, our brother. Cheers."

They clinked glasses.

"By the way, if anyone refers to you as Angelo Dundee, just go with it."

"Holy mackerel, what the heck do we know about cornering, Jimmy?"

"First of all, they call them 'seconds' over here, and we're about to find out." Jimmy raised his beer mug and said, "Angelo Dundee."

"Ya gotta love this man's Air Corps, Jimmy . . . Dundee."

They laughed and ordered another round of beer.

The first couple of fights were a rough beginning, but nobody seemed to notice. If they did, no negativity got passed around. As the fights went on, the boys drew from their experience at the A.C. boxing gym back home and became half decent at "seconding."

The fights continued for months. The Dundee brothers' reputation grew and fighters actually requested them. The boys loved their assignment. A few weeks later, Jimmy was sent off on a new assignment. Angelo found another partner and continued seconding. One morning, as he was about to warm up his fighter, a tough welterweight named Tony Stockton, the CO's office issued a summons.

"At ease. Please sit, Private."

Angelo took a seat, uneasily.

"There's no easy way to say this. I'm sorry, your mother passed away."

Angelo put his face in his hands. "But she was in good health—what happened?"

"Apparently, she was shopping and was struck by an automobile. She was rushed to the hospital but, ah, didn't make it. I'm sorry, Angelo. You'll be given a five-day leave and I've ordered Jimmy back so you two can grieve together. Again, I'm sorry."

Back at what the boys called "the hut," Angelo lay on his bunk. Johnny, his black friend from Atlanta, sat on the opposite bunk and consoled him. "Lost my mother too. Before I deployed. Lung cancer. It's gonna hurt forever but ya learn to live with it . . . sorta."

"I know it sounds screwy but I feel responsible. I coulda put in for assignment at the base near my home—it wasn't mandatory that I join the Air Corps. If I'd been shopping with her I could have seen the car coming."

"That's bull crap. They wouldn't have granted it to you. You white, but you Italian, which means you here with us other minorities."

"You're probably right."

"When's Jimmy coming back?"

"Tomorrow."

From across the barrack, Barrie approached slowly. Johnny saw him and tensed up. Angelo sat upright. If Barrie said anything ignorant, he was about to get his block knocked off. Barrie stopped in front of them, nodded a greeting to Johnny, and then spoke so both of them could hear.

"Hey, Angelo, I ain't looking for trouble. I just wanted to say sorry. I heard about yer mamma. Ah, my condolences."

"Thanks, Barrie. I appreciate that."

Barrie nodded awkwardly and shuffled away.

Jimmy showed up the next morning. The two boys spent the next days of their leave drinking beer, and laughing and crying over stories of their beloved mother. At the end of the five days, they hugged goodbye and Jimmy returned to his base.

Over time, Angelo found a way to live with the pain. But after the tragedy, he felt a need to do more with his life. He decided that in order to truly help his country he needed to be closer to the front. Organizing artillery was not enough, and seconding fights was playtime. He wanted to show his manhood and pay his dues.

He became friendly with a few of the pilots and convinced

them to let him accompany them on drops to their guys near the front. Angelo welcomed the change from everyday base life. He became accustomed to the routine and the C-47 cargo planes' flight path. They'd circle a designated area one time, and Angelo would lean out and wave to the men below. Once they waved back, that was the signal to push out the para-packs. Angelo loved it. The work made him feel like a bigger part of the team.

On Angelo's fourth mission, something seemed odd. He waved at the ground forces but they didn't wave back. Edging forward in the hold for a closer look, the ground troops opened fire. A hail of bullets ripped into the aircraft. Angelo dove backward and fell hard on his tailbone. The pilot banked the plane and turned back toward base. Angelo scrambled back to the hatch. Immediately, he recognized the ground troop uniforms as German. He hauled the hatch closed with all the force he could muster. Catching his breath, he noticed a bullet hole mere inches from where his head had been.

Because of this near-death experience, Angelo received extra points on his record, which would help speed up his discharge. But as it turned out, he didn't need the points. Eight weeks after his last flight, the Third Reich surrendered—the war in Europe was over. Angelo was sent to Erlangen, Germany, to ride out his time, getting some R and R, and enjoying wonderful beer.

In early 1946, Angelo Mirena, also known as Angelo Dundee, landed back on US soil.

Back in South Philly, Angelo's family and friends made a big deal of his return, as they did with every soldier's homecoming. Gas was now fifteen cents a gallon. The average wage was $2,500 a year. It was great to be back with family and friends, yet it was bittersweet. The house seemed so much quieter without their mother in it—as if the very light of the house had been dimmed.

This was not the only sadness to blemish Angelo's return. His fiancée, Rita Carlone, no longer held the title. She'd broken off the engagement and married another man. He'd received the "dear John" letter while stationed in Germany, but it hadn't mentioned her recent marriage, just that she had moved on.

One afternoon, Angelo wandered into the bedroom where Frankie was relaxing and decided to get to the bottom of things. "When did this happen, Frankie?"

"A couple weeks back. We don't know much about the fella, just that they'd been seen around together the last six months or so."

"Ain't that a kick in the gut," Angelo mumbled.

"Any dame that don't wait for a guy in the fight, especially a guy like you, ain't worth two nickels. Try not to let it get you down," Frankie said, putting an arm around his shoulder. "I know it's easy for me to say but—" Frankie let his words drift.

The two men sat in silence until Frankie asked if Angelo would go to see Rita.

"I don't see the point, Frankie. She made her choice, why not let her live her life?" He paused. "Her new life."

The brothers sat another moment until their father came into the bedroom to check on the boys. After adding a condolence of his own, Angelo Sr. asked the boys to return downstairs to the dinner they'd put together in Angelo's honor. It turned out that Angelo's sisters, Mary and Josephine, were darned good cooks. They'd obviously learned a thing or two from their mother. As Angelo's belly warmed with all of his favorite foods, his heart warmed at being reunited with family.

~

Life in South Philly resumed; some routines old, some new. Angelo reconnected with the Rio Boys. It turned out Angelo wasn't the only one in the group to join the fight. Meeting and greeting and getting to know others again, Angelo also reconnected with his previous dance life. This time, he didn't fall for the first dance partner he twirled on the dance floor. Instead, he flirted with a handful of pretty girls.

Now that he was also out of a job, he dug into the search for a career.

By this time, the second-oldest brother of the family, Chris, had made a big name for himself as a boxing promoter. Chris was well aware of his little brother's corner work in England, as well as his clerical skills.

"Well, little brother, are you married to that dance floor or do you want to make an honest buck?" Chris asked during one phone call.

"I've never shied away from hard work, you know me."

"Life is different here; it's a lot faster. Same goes with the fight game. The money's nothing to write home about—not yet, anyway."

"That's okay. Count me in, and thank you for the opportunity."

"Pack a bag and get yourself a bus ticket. You're moving to the Big Apple."

Although Angelo hadn't noticed, he was actually dancing and spinning with excitement while talking with his brother. He hung up the phone, picked up his sister Josephine, and spun her around in the air.

"I'm going to the Big Apple! New York City, here I come!"

"Put me down," his sister protested, laughing along. Angelo

ran to his father, hugged him, and gave him a big kiss on the cheek.

"I'm gonna be working the fight game, Pop! The fight game! Look out, Madison Square Garden."

His father's eyes teared up. Angelo's followed suit. His sister was already crying through her laughter.

Everyone in America had heard fantastic stories about New York. Angelo had also seen a handful of movies. But nothing beat the real thing. If New York and her fight scene was a candy store, then Angelo was a kid knee-deep in it. He could walk for hours on Friday nights, staring at the vast marquee signs lit with thousands of flashing bulbs that advertised movies, plays, and the latest goods America had to offer.

He didn't have the money to venture into these tempting places, but still felt as though he was in proximity to the big leagues. Soon, Chris offered him a job as assistant. Even though the job was more accurately a "go-fer" job—go for this, go for that—Angelo didn't mind.

Chris was on his phone constantly, setting up fights. He had a good reputation for being reliable and making good match-ups. Angelo soaked up the information like a sponge. He learned early on that when Chris's voice took on a certain level tone and he repeated himself, then *that* specific fight was going to happen. Angelo would immediately jot down the information and begin whatever it took to bring the event to fruition.

Chris would hop off the phone just long enough to call out, "Did you get that, Ang?"

"Got it."

"Good. Make it happen and—"

"Make sure we don't double-book anything. Got it."

Seconds later, Angelo would hear his brother dialing the phone to put that fight in motion. Then he would double back and resume setting up two or three other fights. It was a glorious time. The workdays flew by. Most often they worked through lunch without realizing it.

Much as Angelo loved his New York life, the high cost of living was beginning to pinch. Chris had a habit of putting off payday. It wasn't out of malice—Chris was a guy whose right hand often didn't know what the left hand was doing. Angelo would drop subtle hints about how many days had gone by since he'd been paid, but Chris would blow him off.

The day came when Angelo had finally had enough. He was going to give Chris a piece of his mind. He'd walked away from a decent clerical job offer in Philly, darn it, so he wasn't about to work for free. Not for anybody! He wrote the speech in his head and went over it a dozen times before Chris showed up for work. Chris usually barreled in around ten a.m., but this morning he was late. It was enough to make Angelo think twice about the confrontation. Maybe laying into his brother wasn't such a good idea. Sure, he paid late, but he'd given Angelo a break in a city most would only dream about. Growing up, Pop had said, "You love your brothers and your sisters, *capisci*? You love your family. You always show respect to your elders, you always show respect to your family. *Mi capisci?*"

Angelo thought hard on the words. Chris was fifteen years his senior, which meant he really didn't know Chris all that well. He'd left the house by the time Angelo was three. But Chris was his brother, family, so he loved him. Conflicting thoughts spun around and around in his mind. Finally, the clock hit 10:45 a.m. and Chris rolled in. He said a brief hello, then asked for messages. Angelo handed him the slips, then strolled back to his desk, deciding to sit on the money issue for now. During his time of reflection he remembered an old quote: "The Lord helps those who help themselves." It wasn't actually from the Bible, but Angelo liked the sentiment.

He barely slept that night. The next morning he was going to the world-famous Stillman's Gym. Many people said Madison Square Garden was a fighter's dream. That was true to a point, but the fight community also maintained that to train at Stillman's Gym was Christmas and New Year's times ten! Greats like Joe Louis, Sugar Ray Robinson, and Rocky Marciano trained there. It was the place to be.

Angelo sprang out of bed and met Chris for breakfast at a tiny joint called Art's Diner. By rights, Chris should pay. But just in case, Angelo brought enough cash to go Dutch.

After a waitress with a big smile took their order, Chris turned serious.

"When we get to Stillman's, I need you to observe. I want you to listen and learn. There's a lot of hard guys over there, so keep your head down like you always do."

"Got it."

"And whatever you do, don't take what Lou Stillman, the owner, says as personal. He's mean to everybody."

Angelo nodded with nervous excitement. He couldn't wait to step foot in the gym.

"You ever hear about the time Lou went hiking in the woods?"

"No." Angelo leaned forward in the booth.

"He got bit by a rattlesnake—bit him with enough venom to kill a horse."

"Whoa, and he survived?"

"Survived? Ha! After the snake bit him, it slithered away for about ten feet then just up and died. Stillman's blood is that mean!"

Chris sipped his coffee with a stern look on his face. Then he placed his cup on the saucer and burst out laughing.

"Brother, you should see your face," he said. "If only Pop could see you right now."

"So, it's not true. It's an old wives' tale?"

"Yes. Keep in mind that if guys are making up stories like this about a guy, it's not far from reality. So keep that bean of yours down low."

"You don't have to tell me twice. I can't wait to get over there."

"You know another thing about Lou Stillman?"

"On the level this time?" Angelo leaned back and folded his arms.

"Yes, on the level," Chris chuckled. "Lou ain't a Stillman any more than you or I are Dundees."

"No kidding?"

"Lou Ingber is his real name. There was the Marshall Stillman Movement and the Marshall Stillman Athletic Club. When they went their separate ways, the A.C. became Stillman's."

"So why Ingber to Stillman?"

"Since the beginning of time, everyone called him Mr. Stillman and he got tired of correcting everybody. So, the name sorta stuck. No need to bring any of this up, by the way. I'm just trying to educate ya, is all."

"Sure," Angelo said. "I wanna thank you again for all of this, big brother."

"Okay, knock it off. Let's pay this check and make tracks."

They made their way to the gym. Angelo was overwhelmed from the moment he spotted the huge crowd out front.

"What the heck's going on, Chris?" he asked as they crossed the street to the fifty-person-strong crowd.

"They're probably hyping a guy up before a sparring match."

For a sparring match? thought Angeleo. *What do they do before a real fight?*

The crowd was full of smash-nosed, eyebrow-scarred, tough-looking men. They shouted and jostled around a middle-weight-sized man in hand wraps. Chris was correct: they were pumping the guy up. They had to elbow their way through until they reached a large steel door.

"Welcome to Stillman's," Chris said, hauling the door open.

As it clanged shut behind them, Angelo saw they were at the bottom of a steep staircase. The outside noises were dulled and soon replaced by a different sound: the din of fighters. The sounds of skipping ropes, bags being struck, and the shouts of men resounded down the stairs. They started up. With each step, the temperature rose by degrees, as did the smell of a crowded working gym. A bell clanged. It sounded like the beginning of a new chapter to both of their lives.

Reaching the top step, Angelo placed the smell as a blend of sweat, liniment oil, and cheap cigar smoke. He immediately felt at home. They stepped into the hallowed space.

"Hiya, Chris. Who's the kid?"

"Hiya, Jack. This is my kid brother."

"Nice to meet ya, Jack," Angelo said, reaching out a hand. His greeting was cut short by a loud bellow.

"Quit the chit-chat and pay up, ya bums! A half dollar each."

The utterance came from a large man with a cigar stogie in his mouth sitting in a big chair under a giant clock. The three-minute bell sounded again. Angelo quickly dug out fifty cents and paid.

"That Lou Stillman?" Angelo whispered, placing the coins in Jack's big palm.

"The one and only," Jack said.

"Come on," Chris said. "I want you to meet some people."

It was fate, destiny. Everybody seemed to know and like Chris. Some fighters approached to ask about fight representation. It was clear from the get-go that Angelo was being grandfathered into the club, thanks to his big brother. Taking his eyes off of the fighters whose famous faces he recognized, Angelo scanned the fight posters adorning the walls. In between some of the posters were large, empty squares on the walls. For a moment he wondered if some fighters had fallen out of favor and their posters had been removed, but upon closer inspection, he discovered that the squares were windows, covered in thick grime from top to bottom.

Chris caught Angelo staring. "Those have never been opened, little brother."

The bell sounded again. Lou Stillman got up from his seat and shouted at two men sparring in the middle ring.

"Get outta my gym, you bums! My grandmother's got better hooks than you losers. Toss 'em out, Jack, and don't refund their money!" And with that he spat on the floor.

A few fighters turned their heads, but for the most part people carried on, business as usual. Angelo made a mental note never to cross the ornery Lou Stillman. Chris tapped him on the shoulder and led the way up to the bleachers. After a quick introduction to a sportswriter, they sat down. As Chris and the writer chatted, Angelo took in every sight and sound.

There were three rings in total. The main ring, ring number one, held the middleweight fighter who had been hyped outside, sparring with another fellow. They were going at it hard and both were highly skilled. The man from outside delivered a hard body shot. Instinctively, Angelo moved with the blow and said, "Did you see that shot?" A sharp-dressed black man nearby heard the comment.

"Yup, nearly caught the liver," the man said.

Angelo turned to the gentleman. "I'm Angelo Dundee." He held out his hand.

"I'm Joe. Nice to meet you."

Angelo's mouth fell open.

"Joe Louis? You're Joe Lou—the champ! I'm your biggest fan. You're actually here, sitting right here. Holy mackerel!"

Angelo shook his hand again. Joe Louis smiled and thanked him for the compliment.

"Are you going to be a promoter like your brother?"

"You know Chris?"

"Our paths have crossed."

"I wanted to be a fighter as a kid, but didn't have the stuff. Now I'd like to be a trainer."

"Well, you've come to the right place. They call this place the Mecca of Mayhem and it's always served me well."

"I'll say it has. You're the best there ever was," Angelo beamed.

"I don't know about that, but thank you. My advice is to jump in there with both feet. Hang around, get to know the guys, do some bucket work, and go from there."

"Thanks, champ, that was kinda my plan. Good to know I'm on the right track."

"Best of luck to you, Angelo."

They shook hands one last time. When Chris finished his conversation with the sportswriter, he tipped his hat to Joe Louis, who in turn tipped his.

That first day at Stillman's Gym, the center of the boxing

universe, changed Angelo's life. He began training when he could, hanging out, and offering up his services as cornerman or even bucket boy to a handful of fighters. Over time, a few fighters took Angelo up on his offer and paid him ten dollars per fight to corner. Every little bit helped.

Soon, Chris gave Angelo a shot at working Madison Square Garden. Sure, it was as bucket boy, but he rejoiced at the opportunity to "bucket" at the world-famous garden. Angelo was so nervous, he nearly upchucked into his own bucket. He'd never seen nor heard such a rowdy crowd.

At one point he rushed in too quickly to get the bucket down and spilled some of the water. This could be treacherous for a fighter. No way did Angelo want to be responsible for a slip. He frantically wiped up the spill with one hand while steadying the bucket with the other. Other than a quick glare from the trainer, there were no other consequences and no more slip-ups after that. Angelo made it to the end of the fight and was paid fifteen dollars. The five-dollar bump was because the fight was at the Garden.

Between the employment Chris provided and pick-up corner-and-bucket jobs, Angelo was getting by. A few weeks later, as he was shutting off the office lights off after a long day of assisting Chris with a big heavyweight bout between Jack Cranford and Gino Buonvino, the phone rang. He wasn't going to answer—he was beat—but his conscience prodded him. He flicked the lights back on and hustled to his desk.

"Chris Dundee's office. We're closing up, so ya gotta make it fast."

The voice on the other end was female, alluring, and breathy.

"My name is Helen Bolton. I'm Jack Cranford's cousin and I'd like three ringside seats, please."

There had been calls from four supposed Cranford cousins, two brothers, four uncles, and a pastor—and that was just in the past hour!

"Yes, and I'm Jack's grandfather," Angelo sighed. "Look, lady, it's been a long day, the fight is tomorrow night, and I've heard from just about twenty of Jack's so-called relatives. Can you give me break here?"

"But I'm telling the truth, we're cousins. He told me to call this number and it would be no problem."

"I'm about to close. Was there anything else, lady?"

"Are you always this rude to your customers?"

Suddenly he felt bad. He didn't believe this woman but maybe he had been a little snippy with her.

"Three tickets, you say?"

"Yes, ringside, please."

"They'll be at will call, Miss Bolton."

"Thank you and good evening."

Chuckling, he made a note to give this fake cousin three seats way up in the nosebleed section.

The fight was decent. Cranford got taken out by Buonvino in the sixth. Oddsmakers covered their bets. After the bout, Chris, Angelo, and a few others went over to Jack Dempsey's bar, one of the usual hangouts after a big fight. Jack launched into one of his many great stories from times gone by.

Angelo could have listened all night, even to the tales he'd heard before. That was until the most beautiful woman he'd ever laid eyes on walked in with Cranford. The champ had a real looker on his right arm but the one on the left made Angelo catch his breath. Also, her arm was not locked with the champ.

Cranford moved slowly through the throng and thanked

all condolence-givers on his loss. Jack Dempsey's story faded into the background as the mystery lady drew closer. Angelo was standing spellbound beside Chris, Chickie Ferrara, and Jack Dempsey as Cranford and the two ladies stepped up. Introductions went around the group.

"And this fine lady is my cousin, Helen. Helen, this is Angelo Dundee. He's the guy who booked your seats."

"Did you say he was the little brother 'cause he's short? Or just younger?" Helen shot from the lip with her eyes veiled. Those were the most deadly bedroom eyes that Angelo had ever seen and wanted to know better. He cleared his throat.

"Miss Bolton, I'm so sorry about the mix-up—with your seats, I mean."

"I heard about the conversation," Cranford said. "Not your warmest customer service."

Chris threw Angelo a hard look but said nothing. He directed his attention to the champ. "Mr. Cranford, Miss Bolton, please. The first round is on me. I'm so sorry."

Helen accepted, and moved to the table they had reserved. Angelo practically sprinted to the bar, then realized he hadn't asked what Helen wanted to drink. He spun on his heel and returned to the table. The tension seemed to have passed. Cranford was surprisingly cheery. Chris and Chickie were into a deep conversation while the ladies chatted casually.

"Sorry to interrupt everyone. What can I get everybody? I'm buying for the table."

The round would tap him out for the night but he didn't care. He didn't need a drink to stare at Helen Bolton. Memorizing everyone's drink, he was turning to go when Chickie called him back to change his drink order. He leaned in and whispered in Angelo's ear.

"It's a loan, pal," he said, as he discreetly slipped Angelo money for the round. He'd probably worn bucket-boy shoes before and knew the cash was not exactly flush.

"Thanks, Chickie, you're a vitamin shot."

The night went on and Angelo did his best to repair his blunder. He conversed with both ladies, slightly slanting his attention to Helen. It wasn't the least surprising to discover her occupation was fashion model. Here he was, the formerly fat kid from South Philly, sharing drinks and gabbing with a bona fide model in New York. *Who'da thought?*

An hour or so into the evening, a newspaper reporter attempted to shoehorn his way into the action. Seeing that Helen was uncomfortable, Angelo politely asked the man to move on. When he didn't, Angelo grabbed his hand in what looked like a handshake between friends, but actually he was bending the reporter's thumb. The move looked peaceful, but Angelo knew it would hurt the reporter.

When the reporter winced, the rest of the table clued into what was happening.

Angelo whispered into the man's ear, "Take it on the heel and toe, pal. We're closed for business."

The reporter moved on with a curse. The champ winked at Angelo as Helen gave a slight smile. Their reactions made Angelo's night—heck, his whole year!

It was only natural that the two began dating. Helen's statuesque frame, standing five-foot-ten, next to Angelo's short stature made quite the sight. Finances could have been an issue since, as a successful model, Helen made money to spare. But Angelo had to work like a dog to make ends meet. As their dates increased over the next months, they came to an agreement that

Helen would pay for most of their outings. Their love grew, and within a year, Helen Bolton agreed to marry Angelo Dundee.

Chapter Two

ALL I NEED IS A SHOT

Bucket-boy duties faded into the past as cornering become second nature to Angelo. He began working as a trainer with some of the younger fighters and caught the "fight trainer's bug" in a big way.

One Saturday at Stillman's Gym, he was working with a young southpaw, training his left hand to perform.

"Okay, Spike, let's do it again. That was good, but I want you pushing off that back foot on your jab—it'll create more heat. Remember, the punch starts in the feet, moves up the body, and ends in a pop right in the other guy's kisser. Let's go."

The young, pimply-faced kid known as Spike attempted another jab but didn't exactly nail it.

"Not quite. Keep at it."

Spike put his hands down. "Come on, I been at this jab all day. When you gonna let me show my shovel punch? It's a beaut."

"Show me a jab, you get the shovel."

"I won't need the jab. Believe me, my shovel punch is TNT in a leather glove."

"I appreciate your confidence, but what do you think is gonna set up the shovel? The jab, that's what. Now, keep at it." Angelo clapped his hands together in an attempt to pump up the fighter. Spike shook his head and turned back to the heavy bag.

As he watched the young fighter take his stance, Angelo sighed and ran a hand through his hair. Chickie Ferrara, well known for his training talent, came up and stood beside him.

"Hiya, Ang."

"Hey, Chickie, how ya doin'?" There was a hint of tiredness in his voice.

"No complaints. Say, you really think that jab is that bad?"

"No, it's good, but I want it to be great. Besides, he telegraphs that shovel punch all the way from St. Louis. Might as well stun a guy first, don't ya think?"

Chickie laughed. "You're right, and you're a patient man. In my day, any boxer whining about jab work would be doing push-ups for a week." He grinned.

"And then another week of jab work when he was done," he and Angelo said in unison.

"Seriously though, you're pretty good with your fighters. Other guys are starting to take notice."

"Is that so?"

"Yeah, it's so. If you want I can give you pointers here and there, as you know I've done all right."

"All right my eye. You're a legend around here, Chickie. Thanks a heap, I'll take all the help I can get!"

"You're gonna do well in this business, but it takes time. There's gonna be way more lows than highs. I ain't trying to scare ya, I'm just givin' you the gospel the way guys used to with me."

"Sure, Chickie."

"Good. Now then, watch what you say to the press and you don't say nothin' to the mob guys." He paused and stared hard at Angelo. "'Cause the mob don't exist."

"Got it."

"You've got talent and potential. You'll do all right, but watch out for the sharks."

"And who might they be?"

Chickie began counting off a list on his fingers. "The promoters, fighters, trainers, cut men, cornermen, newspaper guys, doctors, sanctioning bodies, and those guys I mentioned that don't exist."

"Geez, Chickie, you're darn near outta fingers."

"We're in the entertainment business of blood, my friend and there's plenty of sharks in the water."

"Thanks, Chickie. You nailed everybody but the referees."

"Oh?" he said with eyebrows raised. "Did I forget to mention them?"

Training on the side, Angelo managed to earn an extra twenty-five dollars per week on top of what Chris sporadically paid him. He was invited into the so-called "club," which meant hanging with other trainers and newspaper reporters at New York watering holes. It was like an internship. He kept his head down, mouth shut, and observed the comings and goings like a midnight owl in a tree. His mentorship with Chickie was developing nicely—Angelo regarded him as a walking encyclopedia.

One night, after a small-time local fight, the guys hung out at Dempsey's, directly across from Madison Square Garden. On the way home afterward, Angelo cut through the Bonneville

Hotel. Passing a bank of elevators, he noticed a man in a long coat and trilby hat worn down at an angle. The man glanced up.

The face looked familiar, but Angelo couldn't place it.

"Hey, I know you."

"No, you don't." the man responded.

"Yeah, yeah, I do. Now, where was it?"

The man gave a straight, blank stare with darkness in his eyes. He had a face straight out of the newspapers—renowned mobster and alleged fight fixer Frankie Carbo.

"My mistake, sir. You have a pleasant evening," Angelo recovered. Turning away, he made tracks out of there.

Nice work, Angelo thought to himself. He'd done the one thing Chickie warned him not to do—*holy mackerel*!

Chapter Three

SUN, SAND, AND THE BUSINESS OF BLOOD

Due to a postwar economic bump, New York's skyline underwent a transformation. Buildings made of glass and steel replaced the prewar, terraced-style architecture. Marilyn Monroe did her famous skirt-blowing scene over a subway grate in Manhattan for a movie called *The Seven Year Itch*. And the fight game continued to grow, although the money did not necessarily find its way to Angelo. Part of the problem was that by the early 1950s, television was gaining in popularity and sales, and many fans were staying home to watch the fights. That brought live attendance down.

In addition, Angelo was reluctant to press his struggling fighters for money. Even though the stable was growing, he had developed a bad habit of loaning fighters money or fronting them for equipment and gym fees. Chris had warned him against the practice, as did his mentor, Chickie Ferrara. Every time Angelo heard the standard line "I'll square up next week," he was pushed deeper into the hole.

Chickie's words reverberated in his head. "That big heart of yours is gonna land you in the poorhouse."

It seems everybody knew he was a sweet guy and that translated as a pushover.

On top of this financial burden, Angelo had barely made any headway with his brother's habit of spotty payments. To be fair, not only was live attendance down because of TV, but the New York fight game was fast becoming crowded with other promoters and managers. Angelo could see it happening, but he had faith in Chris, who was always one step ahead of everyone else.

It was Thursday late afternoon, and by some miracle the phones were silent. Angelo was caught up on paperwork. He leaned back in his chair and began working at a kink in the back of his neck as Chris called out. "Ya got a minute? C'mere, will ya?"

Angelo got up and went over to Chris's side of the tiny office. "What's up?"

"You've done well for yourself up 'til now, right? New York treating you good and all that?"

"Sure, Chris," Angelo replied, not liking the start of the conversation. It sounded like a kiss-off was coming. *Oh well*, he thought, *it was a good run.*

"I'm pulling up stakes, movin' the shop to Miami. It's a completely untapped market, not to mention there's a ton of Cuban talent the world has yet to see."

There was no way he could have seen this coming. It wasn't a kiss-off per se, but it still felt like a parting of the ways.

"I don't know what to say, Chris, except that it sounds like you've got it all worked out."

"I do. Most of it, anyway."

"What about your guys here?"

"Keepin' them. No worries, that's what airplanes are for. I'll be bouncing back and forth a lot in the beginning until I put it all together."

Was that a promotion forming on the horizon? Angelo spoke his thought out loud. "Want me to look after your guys up here until you're set up?"

"No, I want you to come with me. Nobody keeps books like you do, believe me. Plus, you'll be able to build a stable of your own down there. We'll build from the ground up. What do ya say?"

"This is a lot. Thank you. I mean, I'd have to talk it over with Helen."

"Of course."

"Can I take a coupla days?"

"A couple," Chris said, reaching for the phone. That indicated the meeting was over.

"One last thing." Now was his moment, now or never. "You gotta be more consistent with your pay periods—with me, I mean. I'm gonna be a husband soon, raising a family, the whole nine. If I'm as good as you say, then I need that check on the regular. Bill collectors don't wait for no one."

Chris smiled. "The Big Apple put some balls on you. It's about time. I'll clean it up, don't you worry, brother," he said, leaning back from the phone. "But take these words to heart—you need to build your stable up. Make a name for yourself. How long you want to be known as 'Chris's little brother'?"

Angelo looked at him quizzically.

"When are you going to show the world who Angelo Dundee is, huh? I know I don't pay so good 'cause I ain't exactly Rockefeller, but maybe you could be. You've been in the game five minutes and already guys like you. More importantly, they respect you."

The words hit right in the middle of the chest like a shot from a Remington rifle—but in a good way.

"I see your point. Hell, you sound like the old man."

"Think about it, nobody handed me nothin' when I got here and I was younger than you. I've given you a start and I don't want nothin' for it, we're brothers," he paused. "Except for you to take your slice of this world."

Angelo fought back tears. He'd never been more proud to be a Mirena-Dundee.

"Thanks. I'll let you know in a coupla days."

"Only a couple, though."

"You got it."

"And, Angelo," Chris said, reaching for the phone to signify the final end to the meeting.

"Yeah?"

"For the love of Ma and Pop, stop lending money to your fighters, you big blockhead!"

That night, Angelo and Helen decided to dine at the Stage Deli, just few blocks from Carnegie Hall. Helen could read Angelo like a book, and knew there was something on his mind. Still, she waited patiently through appetizers and a huge platter of the deli's famous food as her man made nervous small talk.

"You know, you're cute when you want to get something off your chest," she smiled. "Your voice goes up just a little higher. More wine, sweetheart?"

Angelo's shoulders dropped with a sigh. "Ya got me. Chris is moving down to Miami. He and Gerri already have their place on the market. He wants me—*us*—to go. I didn't commit or anything but—"

Helen burst out laughing.

"What's the rumpus, babe?" Angelo asked.

"Silly goose, don't you remember Chris went down to Miami six months ago and put on the 'Brawl on the Beach'?"

"I remember."

"Sweetheart, your memory. I was visiting my aunt and uncle in South Carolina, remember?"

"That's right. You drove down and met up with Chris. I swear, I'm working too much. You loved Miami, didn't you? I remember you couldn't stop talking about it."

"Darling, if you're sweating over how to talk me into Miami, you can stop," said Helen. "I love Miami, used to go every summer and stay with my aunt and uncle. When do we leave?"

"Baby, you are truly the greatest. But are you sure?"

"Yes, I have friends there. If I can work in New York, you know I can get work in Miami. Heck, the sun will do us good too."

Angelo came around to her side of the table and kissed her. He attempted to prolong the kiss but Helen pushed him away, giggling.

"Angie, this is a restaurant!"

When the waiter returned, Helen ordered champagne. Angelo gave her a nervous look but she said, "It's okay, sweetheart, the bubbly's on me."

Angelo made a second move to come around to Helen but she shut him down with a look and a wag of her finger. He sat back down and worked a phony pout onto his face.

～

They fell in love with Miami. The surf was one of the most beautiful sights they'd ever seen. They took evening strolls, making them a ritual when work permitted. Their seventy-five-dollar-per-month apartment was within walking distance of the beach. Life was grand.

Chris introduced Angelo to a lot of people from the moment he entered Miami's 5th Street Gym. With every new man who came in, the common thread was the respect they all showed for Chris. The first week on the job, a short, dark, balding man showed up.

"Ang, I want you to meet the best doctor and cut man in the business, Dr. Ferdie Pacheco. Ferdie, meet my brother. He's gonna be a big-shot trainer one day," said Chris.

The two men hit it off and Angelo didn't waste any time picking Ferdie's brain about his "kit." Every cut man had a special kit for plugging up the holes that gladiators received. There was so much to learn about gauzes, ointments, tape, scissor brands, and sponges.

Late one Friday morning, a tough-looking guy of middleweight size walked in. He held out his hand. "Doug Vaillant. People call me Dougie. I'm from Santiago."

Angelo shook hands with him. "Santiago, huh? We get a lot of Cuban fighters here. Lots of talent from that little island. I've heard your name from some of the guys."

In fact, just the night before Angelo had joked to Helen that he'd call this time in his life "the Cuban Connection." But it wasn't only Cuban fighters Angelo worked with—he dealt with a lot of Caucasian and black fighters as well. If they had talent and worked hard, Angelo worked with them.

The big fighter relaxed a bit. "I want you to be my trainer."

"First we gotta get you moving around so I can have a look at ya," said Angelo.

"Sure. But I gotta tell ya, I got a thing for women, booze, and drugs. That gonna be a problem?"

"Let's hope not. You're not the first fighter in history with those proclivities. Get changed—I need to see what we're working with."

When the fighter was out of earshot Angelo turned to Luis, his young assistant. "You see what we trainers have to deal with? We got a sport where if a guy doesn't know what he's doing or if he's out of shape, he could get seriously hurt. But still some guys treat the sweet science like it's just a passing fancy. It's ludicrous."

After putting the big Cuban through his paces, Angelo liked what he saw and decided to take him on. What Angelo wasn't aware of was that Doug Vaillant had a fight scheduled three weeks out. They had their work cut out for them. As the training schedule progressed, on only one occasion did Doug show up late with booze on his breath.

"Sorry, Ang, I think I'm getting the flu. Can we skip today and pick it up tomorrow?"

"The flu, my eye," said Angelo sternly. "I suppose that's cough medicine on your breath too."

The big man tried to avoid Angelo's eyes.

"Look, Dougie, I'm here, you're here. Suit up, we've got work to do."

Vaillant dragged his big frame to the locker room and came out a while later. Five minutes into the jump-rope warm-up Doug dropped the rope and sprinted to the bathroom. Some of the other fighters chuckled as the sound of Doug vomiting carried throughout the 5th Street Gym.

"Now that that's done," Angelo said to him as he returned, "let's shadowbox, then we'll hit the bag." Turning to the other boxers he called, "Any you guys got a breath mint?"

The gym erupted with laughter as Angelo waved a hand in front of his face.

That evening, as he and Helen strolled along the beach, he recounted the story.

She listened intently and said, "How gross. Are you sure he'll be ready for the fight?"

"It's really up to him. I don't like to judge a guy for his vices . . . but why he chose *this* sport is beyond me. I'll do all I can."

Helen hooked her arm in his. "You're a good man, Mr. Dundee," she said with a smile. They kissed gently and continued their walk.

The fight was in three days and Angelo believed his guy was ready. They had one final hurdle. The fight was five hours north, in Tampa, which meant Vaillant would have three days on his own before the fight. Tampa had all three of Dougie's favorite party items in abundance. Temptation was going to be a problem.

"Luis, are you sure you don't mind going up there and sitting on Dougie for a coupla days?" Angelo asked.

"No problem. I got it."

"Thanks, pal."

The following morning, when Angelo called the hotel room, all was kosher. Luis and the fighter had checked into the hotel, grabbed a bite, then turned in early—no babes, booze, or drugs. Angelo breathed a sigh of relief and reminded Luis about getting the roadwork in and staying away from you-know-what.

The following day, Angelo worked with a handful of fighters

he'd been neglecting due to the Vaillant fight. After work, he drove north to Tampa with the idea of spending a full day there before the fight the following evening.

At the hotel, he knocked on the room door—no answer. He reasoned that they must have gone out for food. He turned to leave, but for some unknown reason, tried the door. It was unlocked. Angelo slowly opened the door.

"You gotta be kidding me!" he shouted at the sight of upended empty bottles, overturned chairs, and food wrappers strewn everywhere. Luis was passed out on the bed. Doug Vaillant was out cold in a lounger.

"Get up, you bums! Get up!"

Luis came out of it first. "Oh, hey, Boss."

"Don't 'hey, boss' me. I sent you here with a job to do. What happened?"

"He got drunk and, well, then I got drunk."

"Pick him up, get him out of his clothes, and get him into that shower. Heck, you can shower together for all I care, but we gotta get *that* guy," he said, pointing a finger, "*sober*, and I mean yesterday!"

Angelo sat down hard in the lounger. As he heard the shower running he realized for the first time that being a trainer was more than just bag work, boxing, and roadwork.

That afternoon and evening was spent loading Vaillant up with gallons of water and coffee. The next day consisted of a short jog, which Luis went on with Doug, then some light-focus pad work and shadowboxing. That evening, Doug Vaillant went on to win the fight by technical knockout.

Back in the locker room, Angelo loosened Doug's hand wraps. "Nice work in there tonight."

"Thanks. Sorry about that little hiccup," Doug said.

"Me too. Sorry about that," Luis added.

"Don't mention it," Angelo said. "I'll see you guys back in Miami. I'm heading back tonight. You've got the room another night." He paused. "Luis, I expect to see you Monday morning."

"Yes, sir."

"What about me?" Doug asked.

"I've been in the fight game a long time. I saw the two dolls ringside you kept making eyes at. I don't expect I'll see you Monday."

"No, I expect you won't at that," the fighter said sheepishly.

Dusk was Angelo's favorite part of the day, and whenever his schedule allowed he went out for walks as evening approached. He held hands with Helen as they walked along the boardwalk, greeting other strollers with a pleasant hello. On this particular night, they came upon an ice-cream stand. Angelo offered to buy a couple of cones but Helen declined, not wanting to spoil dinner. He took her hands in his.

"At the risk of coming across too sappy, I just wanted to thank you again for the way you've stuck by me."

"That's not necessary, sweetie," said Helen.

"Sure it is. This is not only a tough business, it's an up-and-down business. You've been very patient, is all a guy's trying to say."

"You've said it beautifully." She gave him a gentle kiss on the lips. "But it sounds like there's a 'but' coming."

"No, well, sort of. I have to go to Washington for a couple days. I got Jimmy Beecham a fight up there. I've been going out of town a lot lately," he sighed. "I'm sorry. Wish I didn't have to go."

"It's okay, but you're right."

"Right about what?"

"You are coming off kind of sappy," she smiled. "And I love it. I love you."

"I love you too."

They kissed again, enjoying the last blush of sunset.

Jimmy Beecham was a black middleweight born in Philly. Angelo went with him through the usual pre-fight routine: flight, hotel check-in, press, and minimal workout. The following day they made their way to the arena. Angelo cursed himself for not checking the weather forecast before leaving home as a heavy snowstorm blew in, leaving him dressed in light clothing like a Floridian.

Jimmy earned a draw, but Angelo felt he was lucky to get that. Afterward, Jimmy ate a sandwich then announced he was exhausted and going to hit the hay. Angelo was keyed up and going stir crazy, so he walk-ran to Goldie Ahearn's, a popular restaurant and boxing hangout. As he flung the door open, he was met with the raucous sounds of the packed restaurant. *That's more like it*, he thought. As his eyes adjusted, he scanned the scene for a familiar face. A couple of sportswriters were hanging at a table. He was making a beeline for them when he heard his name being called from a booth. It took a moment to recognize the face that went with the "Hey, Dundee." His body temperature rose when he made the connection.

It was Frankie Carbo, hard looking and still "fixing" boxing matches, if the word around the gym was true. In fact, he'd actually been convicted of the crime, and was just recently released.

"Come have a snort with us, will ya?" he said.

Angelo, not wanting to go near the man, was too slow on the uptake with an excuse to brush the mobster off.

"Sure, why not?" he said, forcing cheer into his voice.

Frankie raised his hand and snapped his fingers. No way could the snap be heard over the crowd noise, yet miraculously a waif of a waitress in a tight mini-dress appeared.

"What can I get you, Mr. Carbo?"

"We're set," Frankie said, "but the famous Dundee needs something to lube his joints."

"I'll just have a beer," Angelo said. "Something light will be fine."

"Come on, Dundee, it's on me. Live a little. He'll have a bourbon, Charlotte." Carbo put his eyes back on Angelo. "You want it neat or rocks?"

"Rocks, please, ah, Charlotte. And thanks, Mr. Carbo."

"Frankie."

"Frankie," Angelo nodded.

As Charlotte sashayed through the crowd, it was obvious that Frankie and his two thickly built associates enjoyed the view.

"Your boy got himself a draw," Carbo said.

"Not his best performance, but it beats losing."

"You get a bonus when your guy wins?"

"Nope. I'm just a salaried working stiff."

Charlotte returned with the drink and set it down on a napkin in front of Angelo. He thanked her, then took a healthy pull on the drink even though he wasn't a bourbon guy. He needed to calm his nerves. If Frankie were about to put the squeeze on him to alter a fight he'd need a little courage to turn the offer down. He would never tamper with a fight, no matter what.

"It ain't right," Frankie said, turning back to his guest.

"What's that?"

"A guy should get a little bump in scratch when his guy puts the other guy on the mat."

"It's the business. I'm good with it."

"You're good with it?" Frankie asked, eyes turning cool.

Angelo felt the associates shifting uneasily. He had no idea what was happening. Why couldn't he have had a sandwich and stayed at the hotel like Beecham?

"I mean, I love the business . . . you know, the way it is. That's all."

The three men stared hard but said nothing. With a shaky hand, Angelo picked up his tumbler and drank until the ice cubes hit his face. Gently returning the glass to the table, he looked at his tablemates individually.

"Look, fellas, I didn't mean to offend anybody here. I just—"

"Relax," Frankie said, leaning back into the plush booth cushion. The coolness seemed to drift from his eyes. Angelo was glad of it. "You read what they say about me in the papers?"

"Who's got time to read the papers these days?" Angelo replied, actually hoping for another drink if he were forced to stay.

"Isn't that where you were headed . . . to the ink guys' table, when you slid in here dressed all Florida like that?"

The associates chuckled at the joke. Angelo smiled but didn't respond.

Frankie leaned forward and put his elbows on the table. "It's gotta be tough on Helen, you working all those hours in the gym, no?"

Angelo felt his face flush as his smile slipped away. Here he was, sitting with a guy who ruined the very sport he loved. Now he was bringing Helen into the picture. Was it meant to be some sort of veiled threat? Whatever it was, Angelo was getting frosty. Bullies. He never liked bullies.

"What'sa matter, Dundee?" Frankie asked.

"Yeah, Dundee, what'sa matter?" an associate echoed.

Angelo tried to hold his words back. It was never wise to insult a mobster. Anybody knew that. Still straining to withhold the words, he locked onto Frankie Carbo's eyes with a look inherited from his father. He might come to regret the move, but so be it.

Finally he said, "We can talk boxing, we can talk bourbon, or we can even talk birds and bees if you want, but we don't talk about my wife."

The table went silent. Angelo could no longer hear the restaurant's buzz. He held the mobster's gaze. Frankie gave nothing, didn't flinch an inch. The associates leaned forward like attack dogs straining against leashes. Charlotte returned, but must have sensed the tension and retreated back into the throng. The three mobsters ignored her movements.

Frankie burst out laughing and was immediately joined by the associates.

"Take it easy, Dundee, you're gonna have a heart attack," he chuckled. "Have another drink, why don't cha?"

Bullies, Angelo thought. *Gee whiz.* "I suppose one more wouldn't hurt," he said with a giant exhale.

Frankie hailed Charlotte and ordered for the table. The threesome returned to their viewing routine. Once the show was over, Frankie, now fully ebullient, turned back to his guest.

"So, seriously, do you read what they say about me in the papers?"

"Ah, *marone*," Angelo said with an exaggerated sweep of his hand. The table erupted with laughter.

Six months later Angelo woke to the ringing telephone. It was David Sykes, a highly respected lawyer and good friend.

"It's kinda early, what's the rumpus?" Angelo asked.

"It's not good. That's why the call at this hour," said David. "You had drinks with Carbo in D.C. after the Beecham fight, yes?"

"Yeah, why?" Angelo felt his scalp begin to heat up.

"The Feds had a wire, a listening device, under the table. They've been watching Carbo since he got out."

"Oh, no."

"What were you thinking?"

"It was just a coupla drinks. We didn't talk about anything. That should be on the tape, right?"

"So far it looks like the Feds think you're just a known associate. Still, the boxing association may not reinstate you. I'll find out as much as I can, but until then don't talk to anyone about this, except Helen, of course."

"Geez Louise, thanks for this. I *knew* I should have stayed in that darn hotel room."

"Isn't that what you usually say to your fighters?"

"I certainly do, David. I certainly do."

Three months went by and Angelo let his New York license lapse, as advised by David Sykes. By the time another three months had passed, Sykes was able to convince the boxing association, based on a letter from the FBI, that Angelo Dundee was barely guilty by association; a guy in the wrong place at the wrong time. He was allowed to renew his license and insisted Sykes send him a bill. But the lawyer would have none of it.

"A word of advice. If you see mobsters in a sandbox, don't play in that sandbox, 'cause next time I'm charging you double."

"No sandboxes for me, my friend. I'm sticking to the ring!"

"Say hi to Helen for me."

"Will do. Thanks, pal."

Angelo's reputation as a decent trainer grew as fast as the Miami setup. With the exception of money being tight, the marriage was going gangbusters. The newfound profession was going well, and it looked even better the day a certain boxer walked into the gym.

"My name is Sam Gentry, and this is Carmen Basilio."

The two men shook hands.

"You don't need to tell me who this is," said Angelo. "It's a pleasure to meet you, Carmen. You must have had over twenty fights in New York. Darn if I didn't miss but one or two of them." Angelo knew he was smiling too much but didn't care. "Did you just come in to look around the place or do you want get a workout in?"

"I've got that fight coming up," Carmen said. "Heard of it?"

"You bet."

"We need a hand in the ring," he said softly. "On fight night."

"You need a bucket boy? I'm happy to do it for you. Whatever you need."

"Ah, no, I need a trainer. I've heard good things about you and from a lot of guys in different places."

Angelo stood speechless. From the expression on Carmen's

face he knew this was no put-on. He straightened up his posture and smartened his look.

"I just assumed that Sam here was the trainer."

Sam grinned. "Nope, I plug him up when he bleeds. I'm the cut man."

Once again, Angelo was at a loss for words.

"So will ya do it? We ain't sayin' it's permanent, but my boy Carmen is going to be the next middleweight champion of the world. Will ya help us get there? Like I said, it ain't permanent, but ya never know."

"Of course I'll do it. We can start right now. Did you bring your gear?"

Angelo knuckled down and studied Basilio's style. Right off the bat, he recognized the unorthodox stance Carmen used. The young trainer was not bothered by the stance because they could use it against an opponent. Many fighters were not comfortable with what was foreign to them, and this could be used against them. Angelo was also aware that Carmen was not the hardest hitter in the game. But what he lacked in power he made up for in toughness and stamina. The man had an iron chin. They both knew that many belts had been wrapped around the waists of boxers without heavy hands.

"On the level, Ang," Sam said. "Are you concerned that Carmen ain't a big power puncher? Do you think he can be champ one day?"

Angelo watched Carmen shadowbox for a moment before turning to the cut man. "Sam, my friend, there is more to boxing than packing the biggest punch. That's why they call it the sweet science. It's a science, and that's why I love this sport."

"You don't know how happy I am to hear you say that."

Angelo steered Sam away from the fighter's workout. Lowering his voice to a whisper, he confided, "No more negative talk or airing insecurities in front of the fighter, you got it? Fighters are the toughest guys on the planet, but they can be fragile. We're talking morale and ego here, *capisci*?"

Sam nodded his head.

"Only the positive, my friend. Just the positive."

Carmen Basilio went on to win the fight, and Angelo gained the full-time position as trainer. The two men knocked down opponent after opponent over the next couple of years, pushing Basilio ever closer to a title shot.

During one regular Saturday morning workout, Angelo noticed Carmen wasn't himself. He lacked pep and was almost listless.

"Okay, okay, timeout. Hang on a second. Carmen, what's the matter with you today? You're dragging out there."

Carmen took his gloves off and faced Angelo. "I just can't catch a break."

"Meaning what?" Angelo asked.

"I'm out here grinding, taking on all comers, and they won't give me a title shot."

"Okay, wait, you say you want a break? Well, this is boxing and in boxing there are almost never breaks," he paused. "For anybody. You've got to beat all the guys they put in front of you and then they tap your shoulder—that's it."

Carmen stepped forward and began counting on his hand of wrapped fingers. "Langlois in April last year. Scortichini in May," he continued counting. "Andrews in June, and don't forget Flore in August."

"Actually, it was September," Angelo said. "You beat Harper in August."

"Whatever, I still won. Add to that Gronik, Harper a second time." he paused, turning away from Angelo. "I mean, come on, Ang, this ain't right."

Angelo was quiet a moment and watched his fighter pace around the ring. He knew his guy needed a moment. Finally he said, "Look, Carmen, we've got Mueller coming up. You stop Mueller and I guarantee the Federation will give you your title shot. We are so close, I can taste it. I've been here before."

Carmen reached down and began putting his gloves back on. "I sure hope you're right, Ang, I really do."

Chapter Four

TIME WITH CASSIUS CLAY, HEAVYWEIGHT CHAMP

The years rolled by for the Dundees. August 24, 1954, would mark the second greatest day of Angelo's life. Helen was in her last month of pregnancy and they were waiting for the blessed event.

One evening while cooking supper, Helen turned off the stove and said very calmly, "It's time." Angelo quickly looked up at her. "Grab my bag, will you, please?" she said.

"It's time? You mean now? The baby—"

"The bag, honey. Let's go."

Angelo was prepared for the baby's arrival—more prepared than his fighters before a fight. Helen's bag sat packed beside the front door. Angelo ran it down to the car and came back for Helen. He gently took her arm. She said she didn't need the assistance but finally relented.

"You're so cute when you're under pressure," she said, getting into the car.

"I don't know how you can be so calm. We're having a baby, for heaven's sake!"

"*We're* having a baby?"

Angelo couldn't believe she could joke at a time like this. He drove ten miles an hour over the speed limit. Every red light threatened to send him over the edge.

"Everything's going to be fine. Just drive like you normally do."

"I'm supposed to be the one calming you down, not the other way around," Angelo said, wiping sweat from his brow. Ten minutes later they arrived at the hospital, safe and sound.

Three hours later, their son, Jimmy Steven, was born.

By this time, Angelo had become good friends with many boxing greats, and they all knew Helen was expecting. A petite nurse in a crisp white uniform called Angelo to the desk telephone at the reception area.

A familiar voice said, "Has it happened yet, Ang?"

Angelo's mind raced to place the voice. "Jake? Jake LaMotta?"

"That would be me," the voice chuckled. "What's going on over there?"

"It's a boy," Angelo said, beaming into the phone.

"No kidding. Congratulations, pal. Me and Vickie, we're close by, but we gotta make a stop first."

"Your cigar will be waiting."

"It better not be a cheap one, either," Jake teased.

Angelo went back to the room and gently took the baby boy in his arms. Helen gave him a fatigued smile.

"Would you look at this kid? He's gorgeous! Thank God he's got your looks, Helen."

"Stop playing, he looks just like his daddy, only a teeny bit more handsome."

"Look at these hands. I think we have a boxer in the family. Yes, I do, yes, I do."

"That kid's not going anywhere near the ring. Give him back to his mother before you corrupt him."

The door burst open and in flew Jake LaMotta with a huge bouquet of flowers.

"Sorry we're late. I told you we hadda stop. Come on in, Vickie. Here, hand me those flowers."

"Geez, Jake, did you rob the flower shop?"

"This ain't nothin'. I paid a guy downstairs five bucks to bring up the rest."

As if on cue, a skinny young man of about twenty entered with two more giant bouquets.

"Put 'em there, kid, and go grab the rest, will ya? Make it snappy."

"Jake, you shouldn't have," Angelo said as he kissed Vickie.

"Never mind all that. Is that the future champ?"

"Yup, come meet Jimmy. Only Helen says he's not going near the ring."

"In a pig's eye he's not. Look at those mitts. Me and you, Ang, we're gonna train him together."

"Don't make me get out of this bed, LaMotta," Helen warned. "You've fought a lot of guys but you've never taken on an angry mother."

"Okay, okay," Jake said, raising his hands in defeat. "We'll work out the details later," he whispered with a wink to Angelo. The kid returned with two more massive bouquets and was followed by another boy around the same age who brought in two more bunches of flowers.

"Thank you, but isn't this a bit much?" Helen said.

"Anything for my godson. You're making me godfather, ain't ya?"

"Jake!" Vickie burst out.

Angelo fumbled for words. "We just, ah, we haven't—"

"What? Ya got a stutter all of a sudden, Ang? Don't worry about it, I'm just jerking your chain. Where them cigars at?"

Angelo reached inside his breast pocket. "Helen, do you mind if we step out?"

"Not at all. I could use the peace and quiet."

"Here, here," Vickie laughed.

Angelo and Jake headed for the door.

"You boys play nice now, ya hear?" Helen said to their backs.

Angelo didn't get nearly as much time as he wanted to spend with Helen and Jimmy. The demands of the job kept him on the road even more now than in his early days. The road was a necessary evil because food needed to be put on the table and bills needed to be paid. Angelo sat at his round kitchen table. Even though it was covered with a red-and-white checkered tablecloth, he still used a coaster for his beer. He admired Helen as she brought plates to the table.

She wore a burgundy dress with a sheer black crinoline beneath that pushed the dress out just slightly. At her slim waist she wore a solid black belt with a large buckle in the center. Her black low-heeled pumps made a pleasing clip-clop as she walked. Her brunette locks flowed down to her shoulders. Over the dress, she wore a cream-colored apron with an image of Rosie the Riveter on the front.

Placing a plate in front of Angelo, she smiled and said his name.

"Yes, dear?" Angelo said.

"You're staring."

70

"Why, yes I am, you beautiful thing, you."

He reached for her but she playfully slapped his hand away.

"You behave, Mr. Dundee," she said, joining him at the table.

They bowed their heads as Angelo said grace.

"Amen," they said in unison when he was done.

Helen picked up a plate but Angelo stood, insisting on serving her. With plates filled, they began to eat with pleasure.

"Last night when you called from Louisville, you said you'd met an interesting character. Tell me about him," Helen said.

"Oh, it was crazy. This kid comes up to me after the fight and gives my guy the usual congratulations. But then he walks with us, talking a mile a minute. And would you believe it, he had all kinds of stats—and not just on my fighters but on *me*."

"Of course, I can believe it. You're good at what you do and people are starting to notice." She stroked his hand gently.

"Thanks, doll."

"So is he a fighter or a fan?"

"Definitely a fighter. He wouldn't stop talking about himself. Just like every other boxer on the planet—"

"Let me guess," Helen said, putting her cutlery down. "He's going to be the next whatever-weight champion of the world."

"Ha, it was like you were there," Angelo laughed.

"Was he obnoxious or a fun distraction?"

"He's certainly confident, maybe over-confident, but he wasn't obnoxious, no," Angelo said, looking to the ceiling as he recalled the memory. "To be honest, the kid's energy was infectious. I liked him."

"Italian fighter? Irish?"

"A good-looking black kid."

"What's his name?"

"Cassius, somebody, Clay. Yeah, Cassius Clay."

"That's an interesting name."

"If he punches as fast his mouth moves, he'll be a force to be reckoned with."

"Sounds like a hoot."

"That he was," Angelo said, taking a sip of beer. Helen put a second pork chop on his plate without Angelo asking for it.

"Thank you, sweetheart, you're a mind reader."

Angelo managed to balance his time between fighters almost perfectly. He didn't want to neglect any fighter, nor did he want them feeling neglected. On top of this, he needed the money they produced, as Chris continued to be sporadic with his pay-checks. However, he had to admit he was giving Carmen Basilio a little extra attention because, by this time, Carmen was inches away from a title fight.

"How you feeling, Carmen?" Angelo asked.

"I'm okay."

"Glad to hear it, because if you win the next one, you'll be the number-one contender—and you know what that means."

"Sure I do, but I won't be number-one contender for long."

"Meaning what?" Angelo asked with a frown.

"Meaning, I'll only be number-one contender until I take the belt from Tony DeMarco. That's exactly what I'm going to do. Then the next guy can be number-one contender. But I'll take him out and anybody else tries to take my belt."

"Now I follow. You'll be number-one contender for a minute but champ for years to come, that it?"

"Bingo."

"I like where your head's at, but we gotta take this one fight at a time, one round at a time. Are ya with me?"

"I'm with ya. Now, are we gonna talk all day or get to work?" Carmen said, faking a kidney shot to his trainer.

"As much as you like the sound of my voice, we're going to start with footwork. With good footwork, he can't hit what ain't there. Then we're gonna toughen up those stomach muscles, 'cause this next guy likes to work the body."

"Sounds like a winner, Ang."

It was the make-or-break fight for Carmen. They were back in Louisville, holed up in a small hotel room, killing time. They'd both had a decent meal and were relaxing with full bellies.

"Carmen, I'm gonna head down and call my wife from the house phone. Can I trust you'll stay out of trouble a moment?"

"How much mess can I get into watching the tube?"

"All right, I'll be right back."

"Tell Helen I said hello, will ya?"

"You bet," Angelo said, closing the door behind him.

Heading downstairs, he considered whether he should have made the "stay out of trouble" comment to his guy. Carmen was a good kid, but fighters who worked as hard as Carmen and obeyed the "no messing with women while training" policy tended to get antsy before a bout. Mandatory alone time with their trainer, cooped up in a tiny room, led many a boxer to climb the walls.

Helen eagerly took his call and listened intently to his little updates. The sound of his wife's voice was a breath of fresh air. Putting the receiver down, Angelo turned to see none other than Cassius Clay, the talkative young boxer. He was wearing a cream-colored, short-sleeved button-up shirt with dark slacks. Beside him was a man wearing similar attire. Both men grinned in greeting.

"Hello there, remember me?" Clay asked, adopting a boxer's stance while biting his lower lip. He appeared to be posing for a fight poster.

"Sure! How are ya?"

"I'm great. This is my brother, Rudy, another fine fighter in the Clay family." He patted his brother on the back.

Angelo shook hands.

Without wasting a moment Clay said, "You've got the great Carmen Basilio upstairs, don't you?"

"Why do you ask?"

"Any chance we could meet him? We're big fans."

"I don't know, fellas, he's got a fight to focus on."

"How about a quick autograph and we'll be on our way. He's going to be champ real soon, same as Rudy and me one day. We all gonna be champs, so what do you say? Two minutes of your time. I'm so fast, I'll be in and out of that room before the ink dries on the autograph. Carmen will say, 'Hey, Angelo, weren't there some fine-lookin' brothers here a second ago?'"

The kid had stones! Still, Angelo liked him and couldn't help but chuckle. How could he deny the kid, with all that charm and mile-wide smile?

"Slow down a minute, kid. Lemme call up and see if he'll take you guys. I ain't making any promises. It's up to him."

"Yes, sir, Mr. Dundee."

"Go back to calling me Angelo, would ya, pal?"

"Yes, sir, Angelooooooo!" Cassius said, putting a melody to the name.

A quick call revealed that Carmen was bored to tears by the television and would welcome the diversion.

"Two minutes tops, are we clear?" Angelo said.

Both brothers nodded, with ear-to-ear smiles.

At the door, quick introductions were made and Carmen invited the lads into the tiny room. They sat and chatted about boxing, boxing, and more boxing. Cassius impressed everyone with his boxing knowledge. Two minutes came and went without an attempt to leave. Carmen seemed happy to rap all night. Two hours later, Angelo insisted the Clay brothers make their exit as Carmen needed his rest. A quick autograph session followed with Cassius making jokes, then handshakes went around the room. Angelo practically pushed them out the door. Cassius could be heard talking through the door all the way to the elevator.

"Coupla class guys right there," Carmen commented.

"Agreed. Now get some rest, future champ. Big day tomorrow."

The next day Carmen won the bout. Both fighter and trainer couldn't have been more pleased. Two days later, Angelo parked his car and walked across the street to Jerry's newsstand, a regular stop on most days.

"Morning, Jer, what's new in the world?"

"You tell me, you're the one making headlines," Jerry said, handing over the *Miami Herald*.

Angelo handed Jerry a dime then scanned the front page. "Look at that, Josephine Baker's coming to Miami."

"Let's hope they let her perform," Jerry said in a low tone. They had spoken in the past about their dislike of segregation.

"Well," Angelo said, folding the paper under his arm, "if she pulls it off, at least it means we're moving in the right direction."

"I hear, ya. Have a nice day."

Angelo crossed the street and pushed the gym doors open. He greeted one of the young guys who was sweeping the floor and then settled into the paper. He scanned a few front-page articles, then jumped to sports until he landed on boxing. All the sports journalists were known to him, and he was halfway through an article when Carmen and his cut man, Sam Gentry, walked in. Both men seemed upbeat—ready to get to work. They exchanged a quick "good morning" before Angelo jumped out of his seat, sending sections of the paper flying.

"Ha ha, look at this, will ya, Carmen? Both Mike Katz and Vinnie 'the Chin' Pepe not only have you as the number-one contender, but both are demanding the boxing federation give you the shot at the welterweight title!"

Angelo tossed the remains of the newspaper over his shoulder and gave Carmen a big hug.

"It's as good as done, my friend. These guys got more influence than the mob."

After they were done laughing, Carmen's face turned serious. "Keep in mind, there is no mob."

All three men were silent a beat until they all burst out laughing again.

By the end of the day, the announcement was made: Tony DeMarco accepted the fight from the challenger Carmen Basilio. The gym was abuzz all afternoon. Congratulations rang out from every corner.

Up until this point in his career, Angelo preferred to keep Helen away from the fight game. Stories around the dinner table were as close as she needed to be, in his opinion. The game was blood, sweat, tears, and corruption; why expose Helen to all that?

But this was a first shot at the title! A dozen wild horses

couldn't keep Helen away. So it was decided that she and her cousin would attend.

". . . and, Dundee, if you're thinking of putting me in the nosebleed seats, I'll leave ya for the milkman, and don't think he hasn't asked," she teased.

"Not to worry, my sweet," he answered. "I fixed you up with two seats ringside. And from now on I'll pick up the milk on the way home. That lousy milkman is fired!"

Angelo arrived in Syracuse, New York, on June 9, 1955, the day prior to the DeMarco fight. He stepped into the War Memorial Auditorium and took a deep breath as his eyes moved over the vast arena. It was always a favorite fight spot, not just because of the building's amenities, but for its tribute to military soldiers. He briefly admired some of the plaques and photos, then walked the bleachers for a few dozen rows and a handful of sections before descending to the ring.

Climbing in, he walked to the center. He jumped up and down a few times to test the canvas's rigidity—it satisfied him. Next, he strolled to the ropes and gave them a couple of tugs— just right. He walked the apron, then climbed down and looked up at the ring. Checking out the seats where Helen would be seated, a smile spread across his face. He had a good feeling about the upcoming bout, a very good feeling.

Later, the crew gathered in the dressing room. An electrical charge seemed to course through the room as he got down to business.

"All right, Carmen, you just remember to fight your fight, not his."

Carmen nodded. Angelo knew he was heard, but at the same time his fighter was no doubt moving through the fight in his mind's eye.

"Remember what I told you about this guy, DeMarco. He telegraphs his right hand and you're the faster guy, you can beat him to the punch."

"Okay."

"I want your lead leg close to his body but you need to keep out of range. He'll think you're closer than you actually are, and with your good head movement he'll be swinging at air. Got it?"

Basilio nodded a second time.

"Good. Now, I need you to pay attention to me in between rounds. You'll be all charged up, but stick with the plan and you get the belt. Got it?"

"Yeah, got it."

"Whose belt is it?"

"Mine," Carmen answered.

"I'm sorry, I didn't hear you. Hell, a mouse wouldn'ta heard you. I asked, whose belt is it?"

"Mine!"

"Whose?"

"*Mine.* It's my belt. That belt belongs to me, Carmen Basilio!"

"All right, let's get out there and take what's yours," Angelo shouted. The rest of the crew clapped and cheered Carmen down the tunnel to the ring.

Carmen wore light trunks, while Tony DeMarco wore dark. From the opening bell the two went at each other. Neither one pulled his punches. Carmen was certainly ahead in the early rounds but he had a long night ahead of him. Angelo called commands from the corner. At the end of the sixth, Carmen sat heavily on the stool but his wind was good.

"Carmen, you're doing great. Now listen, you're faster than this guy and he's telegraphing his haymaker just like I said, so here's what I want. When he loads up that right, jab him in the right shoulder. It'll knock him off balance and frustrate him. Frustration leads to mistakes. Nod if you understand. Good. Now get out there—it's your night, it's your belt!"

Three more rounds passed with Carmen still slightly in the lead. But to beat the champ, the win had to be decisive. Carmen implemented Angelo's shoulder jab plan nicely. It often set up Carmen's right cross—Angelo was pleased.

The bell rang. Carmen plopped down on the stool. He was tired, but not as bad as Tony DeMarco.

"We're looking good. You're killing him on the inside. Keep working that body because he ain't blocking bubkes with his elbows. He's giving you a gift, kid. Take it. Take that gift. Punish that rib cage and get that belt!"

Carmen, the bigger man, executed the plan and by the twelfth round the referee stopped the fight. The emcee boomed, "The belt and welterweight crown goes to Carmen Basilio!" Angelo had his first champion!

The hits kept on coming. In 1956, the Chicago Sportswriters and Broadcasters made him Boxing Trainer of the Year. In 1957, Helen gave birth to Terri, their beautiful little girl.

Before long, it was 1960. The Olympics were slated to be held in the alluring city of Rome. Cassius Clay was going for the gold, and it was all being televised for spectators in America. Angelo, Helen, Jimmy, and Terri gathered around the television to watch.

"Who's Cassius fighting, honey?"

"A Polish guy by the name of Zigzy Pietrzykowski."

"Easy for you to say," Helen responded.

"Who wins, Daddy?" Jimmy piped up.

"I believe young Cassius is going to win, Jimmy. He's going to bring the medal home to the States."

"Yay!"

"But we can't celebrate yet, son. Climb up here with Daddy. Good boy."

"Which one is he?"

"He's the black guy in the light trunks. Ooh, did you see that? He sometimes leads with his right hand. Not a lot of guys do that."

"He's scoring points with it too, if you haven't noticed, sweetheart," Helen added.

"You've got that right. See how smart Mommy is?"

"I have Clay winning the first two, honey," Helen said.

"We've got one more round. What does that make, Jimmy?"

"That's easy. Three!"

"When did you get so smart?" Angelo asked, tickling his son. Jimmy laughed and squirmed to get away, but Angelo hung on. Hearing her older brother laugh, Terri joined in. Angelo wrestled and tickled both kids while attempting to view the third and final round.

"Look at the speed, Helen."

"I see it, I see it."

"There's the shuffle everyone's been talking about."

"You mean that quick-footed dancing thing?"

"You bet. Apparently, they eat it up in Louisville."

The final bell rang. They all watched as the ref held up Clay's glove. "The winner!"

The entire family got to their feet and cheered as Clay bounced around the ring, playing to the crowd. Angelo gave Helen a big kiss.

"Another gold for the States," Helen smiled.

"I'd sure like to work with that kid."

"You never know, you just might."

"You never know is right. Did I ever tell you the sage advice I gave him last year?"

"Yes, dear, you told him to go win the gold first before turning pro so his stock would be worth more."

"Ah, a beautiful lady with a steel trap memory, I see," Angelo smiled.

"I wouldn't be surprised if you heard from him, honey."

"Only time will tell."

Cassius Clay turned pro and eventually signed with the Louisville Sponsoring Group, an eleven-man cluster of investors led by William Faversham Jr. Word had gotten to the group that Dundee was the man, the rising star of boxing trainers. That was enough for Cassius Clay. He called to announce he was moving to Miami. Angelo was touched and a little more than excited when he took the call.

"Let me start by saying that I'm honored you've chosen to work with me, Cassius. Oh, and congratulations on your gold!"

"Thank you for making space for me on your roster."

"I'm happy to do it. But ya know, the real hard work begins now that you've decided to go pro. You'll be saying goodbye to three-round fights."

"I know it. I get my roadwork in, I train hard, and I'm a good listener. Some say I talk too much but that don't mean I ain't listenin'."

Angelo chuckled. "Let me grab a pen so I can jot down your flight arrival details. Can ya hang on a minute?"

"Sure thing."

Angelo let the phone dangle on the cord and grabbed a pen

and paper. Now with the phone cradled between his ear and shoulder, he was ready to go.

"Shoot."

"Pan Am flight 357, comin' in tomorrow at two p.m."

"I'll be there to pick you up. Safe travels, Cassius."

"Thank you. I can't wait."

Angelo got a parking spot nice and close to the entrance. As he walked through the doors, Cassius came toward him with a single suitcase.

"Here already?" Angelo said, surprised.

"Plane got here early. I guess the pilot was fast, like me."

The big man put his bag down to shake hands. Cassius had a firm grip—Angelo liked that.

"Welcome to Miami."

"Happy to be here. Where do you have me staying? I'd like to drop my things off, change, and get to work, if that's cool with you."

"It's cool with me, all right but, ah, where you'll be staying is not so cool, I'm afraid."

"What do you mean?"

"I checked into a couple places and they, ah, how can I put this? They turned me down flat when I told them a black man would be renting from them."

Clay sighed heavily. "In other words, they'll accept my gold medal, just not my brown skin."

"Sorry, Clay, racism seems to be alive and well in these parts."

"How you feel about this situation?"

"I saw this crap in the service and I set those knuckleheads straight. Even now, when a sportswriter asks me why I train so many black fighters, I tell them I'll train a Martian if he works hard. The color of a man's skin didn't bother my mother, my father, and it don't bother me nor any Dundee, for that matter."

The young Clay stared hard a moment before speaking.

"I'll accept that," he said picking up his bag. "So where you dumping me?"

"Hop in."

Angelo pulled out of the airport and onto the main drag. Traffic was light. Cassius talked almost constantly as he looked out the window. Angelo glanced over from time to time and could see Clay's cheekbone raised in a near permanent smile.

"It's just like in the movies—palm trees, sunshine, ooh, and look at all of the pretty ladies you have down here."

"Let's focus on the fighting, shall we?"

"I'm focused on the fighting, all right, but I'm peeking at these women."

"As long as that's all you're doing."

Cassius continued to marvel at his new surroundings. Angelo found it refreshing.

"Oh-oh!"

"What's the matter?"

"I'm seeing a change in the landscape. Broken-down cars, garbage on the sidewalk, more liquor stores. Looks suspicious. We just cross a color line?"

"No flies on you. Welcome to Overtown, my friend."

"Seems ghettos are the same all over. Shame."

"I'm truly sorry, Cassius."

"No need to apologize, Mr. Dundee. I may be young but I do know what time it is in America."

Angelo didn't know what to say. He felt horrible. Making a left, he cruised halfway down the block and looked up at a rundown two-story building. The formerly bright butter-yellow building had faded to off-white. A shirtless black man sat on the crooked front steps. He got up when he saw their vehicle.

"Welcome to the Overtown Arms. Will you being staying here?" he said.

Cassius got out of the car. "Where you from, brutha?" he asked.

"Jamaica, man."

The two men smiled and shook hands the way Angelo had seen many black men shake hands.

"I'm Cassius Clay. Nice to meet you."

"Me recognize a gold medalist when me see one. Welcome, me name Byron."

"How many miles is it from the gym?" Clay asked, suddenly turning upbeat.

"I dunno, about five miles, give or take."

"Good, I'll get my roadwork done on the way in to my workouts."

"Sounds like a plan." Angelo was pleased. Most of his guys needed harassing to get their roadwork in.

"I'll draw him a map, Mr. Dundee, every-ting gon' be aw' right," Byron said.

Angelo left so Clay could unpack, then met him back at 5th Street thirty-five minutes later.

"Wow, you made good time. No trouble finding your way back?" Angelo asked.

"It is other men that need direction."

"Oh, brother! Let's go to work."

Over the next several months, Angelo and Cassius got to know each other. Amateur fights went three rounds, so first they focused on Clay's stamina. He had to be ready to go the distance and that meant fifteen rounds; five times what Clay was used to. The good news was Clay loved to train and that included roadwork. Angelo was a stickler for roadwork. He announced many times per day, "I don't care what time of day or night you do it, but ya gotta get your roadwork in, period."

Many fighters protested running, but not Clay. If anything, Angelo had to convince him at times *not* to train.

"Go home, Clay, the gym has been closed thirty minutes already," Angelo would often say.

The beginnings of a friendship formed outside the ring. One Friday, as usual, most of the other fighters had left. Clay was unwrapping his hand tape when Angelo came out of the office and approached the young fighter.

"Got plans tonight?"

"Goin' on a run later, but that's about it. Why?"

"How would you feel about a home-cooked meal? Helen and I want to have you over tonight. That is, if you're free."

"I can't say no to that, Mr. Dundee. What time?"

"How's seven o'clock suit you?"

"Suits me fine."

"Great, I'll pick you up at a quarter to."

"I'll be ready with an empty stomach."

That evening Angelo introduced Clay to his family. "Kids, this is Cassius Clay, the boxer I told you about. Cassius, this little tiger is Jimmy and—"

"And I'm Terri," Angelo's daughter said, sprinting to the door to greet the guest.

"You didn't tell me you had two big teenagers living with you," Clay teased.

"I'm five and she's two, Mr. Clay, we're not teenagers yet," Jimmy said seriously.

"But you're so big, though," Clay said. "You must get your height from your mother."

"Everybody's a comedian," Angelo said, nudging Clay on the shoulder.

"Nice to meet you," Helen said, wiping her hands on her apron before shaking Cassius's hand.

"Oh my heavens, two teenagers and a beauty queen. You can't be Angelo's wife. Did you just stop by to pick up your beauty crown and then you're on your way?"

"Stop it, Mr. Clay, I'll get a swelled head."

"Be honest . . . Angelo brainwashed you, didn't he?"

"Keep it up, Clay, and this will be your last dinner in this house," Angelo warned teasingly.

Jimmy tugged on Clay's pant leg. "Are you the champ?"

"Not yet, but soon, young man. And do you know what else?"

"What?"

"I'm going to be the prettiest heavyweight champion there ever was."

"Ew, boys can't be pretty."

"Really? I didn't know that. Can girls be pretty?"

"Yes, I mean, no. Ew, yuck," Jimmy said, running away. Terri joined in on the laughter. Cassius walked into the kitchen.

"Mrs. Dundee, this all smells amazing. I can't wait to eat."

"Thank you, we'll eat in about thirty minutes."

Clay mock-lowered his voice to a whisper. "Blink twice if you're being held here against your will."

"I heard that," Angelo said as he joined them in the kitchen.

"Tell the truth, now. You kidnapped her from a beauty pageant, didn't you."

"Cassius, you are incorrigible," Helen giggled.

Angelo shook his head with a smile. "I'm having a beer but you're in training . . . so can I get you water, orange juice, or milk?"

"I'll take the milk. They say it's good for the bones. Speaking of bones, you have lovely bone structure, Mrs. Dundee. I think you might be prettier than me."

"Oh, will you knock it off?" Angelo laughed. "You see what I have to deal with day in and day out, Helen? I oughta throw him out of the gym is what I should do."

"Ha, then who's gonna show them other boys how to box? I see how they try and steal all my moves, but the problem is, they're all just so slow. I'm so fast, the sound barrier asks me for advice."

"Now wait a minute, I got some good fighters in my stable," Angelo said, handing Clay a glass of milk.

"Time out," Helen said. "If you're going to talk boxing, you need to take it in the other room."

"We could stay here and talk about how pretty we are, Mrs. Dundee."

Angelo playfully shoved Cassius out of the kitchen and into the living room.

"Careful, I don't want to spill this milk and have you cry about it in front of your kids."

"It's nonstop with you."

The two men talked boxing over numerous interruptions by the children. Angelo admired the way Cassius handled the kids, never seeming bothered. In fact, he teased and played with them to the point where the kids were smitten.

At the dinner table, the men talked boxing until Helen cleared her throat and brought the conversation to a different topic. But like flies to sugar, Angelo and Cassius always meandered back to the sweet science.

When the kids' bedtime rolled around, they insisted that Cassius read their favorite story. They laughed hysterically as he continuously strayed from the story and inserted the kids into the tale.

"You're supposed to be calming them down, not winding them up, Cassius," Angelo chuckled.

When the children were finally asleep, the adults talked for two more hours until Cassius insisted he needed his beauty sleep.

"Because it is not easy bein' this pretty!"

Days passed, and as training continued, Angelo discovered that his fighter liked to think that every good boxing idea or tactic was *his* idea. It wasn't his first time working with this personality type, so he used psychology.

"What was that, Clay? Were you pushing off a little harder with that back foot on the jab? It seemed to add pop to the jab."

The fighter didn't answer, just continued to work the heavy bag. Two rounds later he announced that he'd developed a technique whereby pushing off his back foot gave his jab more power.

Several fights were arranged and Clay won them all. In fact, he fought fifteen fights and won twelve by knockout. On top of this, he took to predicting the round number in which he would defeat his opponents, and was correct 100 percent of the time. These predictions made Angleo uncomfortable at first. In fact, he was uneasy about Clay's braggadocious manner altogether, as it was entirely foreign to the way Angelo had been raised. However, it was infectious. Clay was infectious. The press either loved him or hated him, and either way, they packed venues.

Any time Clay had a microphone in front of him was a magical moment. The genius behind his taunting became evident over time, because he'd get inside the opponent's head before they even entered the ring.

Clay and the Dundees continued enjoying dinners at home.

"Do you know what this means, Clay?" Angelo asked.

"It means when I whoop Archie Moore, I get a title shot at Sonny Liston."

"That's right, but don't take Moore lightly. He may be forty-three years old but he holds the knockout record."

"One hundred and forty one knockouts, I know the stat."

"I'm glad you know, because you've got to respect that big right hand of his. One thing about big heavyweights—as you age, you get a little slower but you don't lose power, *capisci*?"

"Helen, why is your husband always trying to teach me Italian?"

"He's a proud man," Helen said, pinching Angelo's cheek, then giving him a gentle kiss.

"I swear, you put some kind of spell on this lovely, unsuspecting woman."

"Can ya blame me?" Angelo laughed. "But seriously, Clay, back to Moore. An aging lion can be one dangerous animal."

"I hear you, Mr. Dundee."

The table fell silent a moment. Clay turned his napkin over and looked thoughtful.

"I'm still taking him out in four, though."

"*Aduzipazz*!" Angelo said. *You're crazy*!

Angelo had canceled work on Saturday, but needed to briefly drop by the office. He'd almost forgotten it was his daughter

Terri's birthday. Cassius had been invited over and Angelo was pleased when he accepted. "There's always work to do," he told Terri, promising he'd be back in plenty of time for the party.

The office errand took longer than expected, and he was actually thirty minutes late for the big party. He expected to walk into a packed free-for-all of loud kids but there was only Helen and Cassius playing with Jimmy.

"What the heck is going on here?"

Helen explained that the parents of Terri's friends had been calling all morning with apologies. "Since moving to this house we're just too far away."

"What? Nonsense. Where's Terri?"

"In her bedroom crying it out."

Angelo didn't waste any time heading to her bedroom. He gave a gentle knock before letting himself in.

"Hiya, sweetheart, everything okay?"

"No! Nobody likes me," Terri sniffled.

"Not true, not true. Sweetie, I'm afraid this is all my fault. I moved us to this nicer home, not realizing it was so far from your friends. But I have a plan."

Terri looked up from her doll and stared with eyes full of hope at her father. "What plan?"

"Do you still want to have a party?"

"Yes."

"Then you wait right here with Dolly and I'll be back in thirty minutes, okay?"

"Okay."

Angelo hugged her and headed for the door.

Terri spoke before he made his exit. "Daddy?"

"Yes, dear?"

"Her name is Jessica," she said holding up the doll. "Not Dolly."

"Nice to meet you, Jessica. I'll be right back in thirty minutes." He paused. "Maybe make that forty minutes. Sit tight."

Back in the living room Jimmy and Cassius were on the floor playing with Jimmy's fire truck.

"Helen, I'm going to round up all of Terri's friends and bring them back here. You coming, Cassius?"

"No, Mr. Clay is playing trucks," Jimmy said.

"I'm playing trucks, Ang. You're on your own," Cassius said.

"On my own it is. Helen, I love ya. Don't let Clay finish that cake."

"Hey!" Cassius protested.

"How are you going to—" Helen started, then stopped herself. "I'm not even going to ask. Hurry back, Superhero."

Angelo got back to his old neighborhood and went straight to the Stevens residence. Fran Stevens opened the door with a shocked expression when she saw him.

"Fran, grab Stacy and her brother and follow me in my car. You've got a party to go to."

"But—"

"No buts, let's go. Terri's dying to see them."

"Oh, all right, give me a minute."

"I'll swing back by in a minute. I'm going to grab Jerry Crowley and his two girls."

Angelo skipped every other step, ran to his car, and drove to the Crowleys. The daughters were excited the party was back on. The Crowleys followed Angelo back to the Stevens's place, who then followed them over to the Jacksons.

The Jackson boys screamed with excitement, as they'd been

looking forward to the party all week. With the Jacksons in the rear, Angelo led the convoy of vehicles to the Godfreys. Little Tania Godfrey jumped up and down with excitement.

"Holy cow," Bob Godfrey said when he looked out and saw the convoy. Angelo now had a system that with each pickup all cars were to honk their horns. It was, Angelo had to admit, becoming a real hoot!

The convoy made four more stops. Everybody said yes. Forty-five minutes later the convoy rolled up to the Dundee residence.

The party was a hit. Terri hugged her dad like Superman himself had rescued her. The grownups were thrilled to find Cassius Clay at the party, who charmed the guests with nonstop jokes and teasing.

Angelo stood with his arm around Helen's waist and took it all in.

"You did it, Angie, you really did it. You saved the day. Look how happy Terri is."

"She deserves it."

"Should I serve the cake?"

"Nah, let those little maniacs run around a bit more."

The location was Los Angeles, California, and the date was November 15, 1962. Twenty-year-old Cassius Clay stepped into the Sports Arena ring wearing a shiny white robe. He moved around, testing the canvas with quick footwork and his now-famous shuffle. A large portion of the crowd cheered.

Clay was followed in the ring by Archie Moore, who looked to be a much heavier man. Angelo took his spot in the corner and set up shop. Current heavyweight champion Sonny Liston, wearing a handsome dark suit, stepped in and shook hands with both fighters, then waved to the crowd before exiting.

Clay had predicted he would knock Moore out in the fourth round, and the press had eaten it up. The bell tolled. Clay moved forward like a cat, while Moore lumbered. Clay took the fight to Moore and won the round. Round two went almost the same way. Halfway through, Clay hurt Moore with an overhand right.

"That's it!" Angelo shouted.

By the time Clay sat on the stool at the end of the round, there was little to say except, "Moore's gotta know he's behind on points. He'll be coming for you now. Respect that right hand, Clay. Respect it!"

Moore moved forward exactly as Angelo had predicted. He caught Clay with a right but Clay rolled with it, making it look worse than it was. Moore was desperate to land one big bomb— it was the only chance he had with the younger, faster man. The bell tolled again. Clay strode to his corner. Angelo bent low to his ear.

"This is your predicted round. Don't go headhunting. Be smart. Be patient. If it doesn't happen in the fourth, so be it. Don't get caught!"

"I know what I'm doin'."

Angelo clapped him on the shoulder as the bell rang out.

Clay moved into the center of the ring and waited. As Moore moved in, Clay threw lightning-fast jabs and combination punches in dazzling succession until Moore went down. Clay stood over him with hands raised and did a quick shuffle. Moore struggled to his feet only to go down two times more before the referee called the fight.

It was Archie Moore's last fight, and everyone knew it. Clay dashed across the canvas as "Ageless Archie" struggled to regain his feet, and embraced the older fighter warmly. The cameras captured his emotional show of heart, endearing many fight fans to him at that moment.

Angelo was overjoyed. His guy was now going to get his shot at the title. Sonny Liston, watch out! But the win was bittersweet, for it was never pleasant to see an aged warrior shoved aside by a youngster half his age.

There was little time to celebrate. Instead, trainer and fighter dug into the work. When not in the gym, Clay went on the biggest fight-promotion campaign of his short career. He was getting more outrageous for the cameras, shooting from the lip at the microphones. At times, Angelo felt Clay was going too far.

"I just think you should tone it down a bit. Like it or not, Liston is one hell of a fighter. From what I hear, he's mean as a snake. Why ya wanna go poking the bear?"

"An angry bear won't think straight. He'll come in all wild and stick that big chin of his out and I'll be right there to *boom*, put him to sleep." Clay acted his words out as he uttered them, dancing and jabbing. "Besides, he's ugly, and I'm just so pretty."

Angelo sat back, folded his arms, and shook his head. "Ya know, you're building a lot of heat for yourself but you're also making a lot of enemies. You don't want that in this sport, believe me."

"Do you know what I want?"

"What's that?"

"I want what you have, a beautiful wife, beautiful kids." He paused and spread a giant smile on his face. "And I want that beautiful belt around my waist. The sports writers and enemies, they can all jump in a lake, as far as I'm concerned."

Cassius leaned forward on his elbows and beckoned Angelo closer. His trainer leaned in and turned an ear.

"Now, you can join me or stand in the corner, but one way or another this crazy brutha is going to drive that Liston sucka nuts *before* he steps in that ring, and then," he paused for effect, "I'm gonna knock him the hell out!"

"So, there's a method to your madness."

"I be crazy like a fox, Ang. Ca-ray-zee!"

February 25, 1964—fight night! At the Convention Hall in Miami Beach, it was Cassius Clay versus Sonny Liston in the Heavyweight Championship of the World. Clay was the eight-to-one underdog, and just twenty-two years old.

Sonny Liston's biggest weapon was his left hook, so Angelo instructed Clay to move to his left, or clockwise, nullifying the champion's ability to take a shot. The first round went to Clay, due to the speed of his jab and short combinations. The crowd was so raucous that neither fighter heard the bell signaling the end of the round. They fought a full eight seconds past the bell's toll.

In round two, Angelo called to Clay for head movement, which he implemented beautifully. For all the mugging and big-talk out of the ring, there was no mistaking the grace and precision Clay brought when he actually got down to business. As Clay sat down on his stool at the end of the round, a new respect was palpable on the part of the announcers and crowd. Angelo bent low over the stool to hear him.

"He can't touch me. He can't touch me," Clay murmured.

"True, he hasn't touched your head, so now he's coming for your body. Do ya hear me? He's coming for the body. Be ready."

The bell sounded, and on cue, Sonny Liston lunged for Clay's body. But Clay's lightning footwork was no match for the slower Liston. Near the end of the round, Clay landed a devastating left hook to the champion. Liston was hurt. Clay wasted no time delivering a one-two and opened a cut under Liston's eye. Round three went to Clay.

After the fourth round, Angelo sensed a problem. "What's going on? You've turned off the gas?" he asked.

"My eyes, I can't see."

"What?"

"Stinging, they're stinging."

Angelo dug into his lengthy experience. "Lemme see your gloves." He grabbed a clean towel from the cornerman, wiped it over the glove, and then dabbed the corner of the towel into his own eye.

"Son of a gun, that smarts. Get me some water, we gotta flush Clay's eyes, hurry up!"

The men went to work on their fighter. Angelo peered over at Liston's corner. He wanted answers.

"Dang it, I'm too short to see over there," he mumbled, kneeling back down. "How are the eyes, Clay?"

"Blurry."

"Well, it looks like you gotta get on that bicycle and go for a ride until we can flush you again."

"I don't know if I can do that. He knows I can't see. I'll be a sitting duck."

"You get on the bike like I said, and if he sounds close you grab hold and don't let his gloves near your eyes."

"Sounds close? Is that all you got?" Clay asked with wide bloodshot eyes. Clay shook his head back and forth.

"You want me to throw in the towel?"

"Hell no, I'm just trying to shake my vision back."

"Good, nobody quits on this team. Fellas," he turned to the

other cornermen, "another flush quickly. The ref's given us the signal."

Clay did as instructed and danced away from Liston for most of the fifth round. He squinted, attempting to clear his vision. Angelo's own eye still bothered him. He admired Clay's poise—half blind, and surviving against a champ!

At the end of the round, the crew worked diligently on Clay's eyes. When the time came to fight again he gave them a nod and leapt off the stool. The combatants met and Clay delivered his stiffest combinations of the night. The crowd was starting to turn Clay's way. By the time he sat back down on the stool, there was activity in Liston's corner.

"What's that cat doing, Ang?"

Men were bent over Liston with concerned looks.

"That's the doctor. He's going to check. Sit tight."

Soon, the announcement came. The doctor insisted the fight be stopped. Sonny Liston was not coming out of his corner.

Clay won by TKO and was pronounced the new heavyweight champion of the world! Angelo Dundee had himself another grand-slam winner.

Chapter Five

FROM CLAY TO ALI

Cassius Clay did the usual victory lap. He talked to reporters, signed autographs, posed for pictures, and mugged for the TV cameras. The hype showed no sign of abating, so the newly minted champ used security to clear a path toward the exit. Clay and his entourage eventually arrived at Gino's, a simple Italian family joint with the best pizza in town. Angelo, Helen, Chris, and other friends, family, and fighters were all waiting to celebrate.

A roar of cheers and rounds of applause erupted when the new heavyweight champion walked in. Clay shook hands or hugged every single person in the place. At one point he even went back to the kitchen and whipped the staff into a frenzy. Back at the victory table, he picked Angelo up in a bear hug and twirled him around three times before setting him back down.

"I am the greatest! I am the greatest! And Angelo, you're . . . not bad," Clay said. The room roared with laughter. Then Clay stole a piece of pizza off Angelo's plate and talked a mile a minute with his mouth full.

"Hey, you only get one piece! I don't want you ballooning up on me," Angelo warned. The room erupted once again with laughs.

Three waiters walked around with a bottle of Prosecco in each hand, filling everybody's flutes to the brim. When Clay adopted a devilish grin, Angelo knew what was coming but was too slow to evade. Clay grabbed a bottle of the bubbly vino, shook it up, and sprayed him with half the bottle. After taking a big swig, he poured the rest over his head.

Willie Pastrano, the light heavyweight champ in an alternate division and a good friend, grabbed another bottle and went after Clay. Soon other fighters joined in the bubbly battle.

"Buncha kids," Angelo quipped to Helen as he wrung his shirt out, laughing.

"I'm so proud of you," Helen said, kissing Angelo on the cheek. Her clothes were wet too. She'd been caught in the bubbly shower.

"Doll, your sweater."

"No big deal, I'm having so much fun. But you're right, they are a bunch of kids." She chuckled as they looked on at the spectacle.

The next day, Angelo awoke with a slight headache and a smile on his face. He showered, dressed, played with the kids, and then drove to a press conference. On his way inside, several fans met him. He welcomed all of the praise with a giant grin, stopping a few times to chat with some of the sportswriters. Eventually, he took his seat beside Clay.

Moments later the world flipped on its side. Everyone

expected Clay to launch into another entertaining schtick, talking about how he felt, which new fight was his to win, along with liberal praise for his own good looks. Instead, Clay grabbed the microphone and went in a totally different direction. He talked of his faith in Islam and that he believed in Allah, not God. Sitting there, Angelo's head began to spin. He hadn't seen any of this coming.

"I renounce my slave name. From this day forth, I shall be known as Cassius X," the new champ said to the stunned crowd. The reporters went wild, all of them shouting at once. Cassius answered a few questions, then excused himself.

Angelo managed to get him alone in a private room.

"You sure like to shake things up, don't ya, champ?"

"It is what I believe. Are you okay with this?"

"A heads-up would have been nice, but you do what you need to do."

"Thanks for understanding."

The two men were silent for a moment, considering what just happened.

"Can I be frank with ya, Clay, sorry . . . Cassius?"

The fighter nodded.

"I know more than half of those reporters out there and most of them are decent guys. But I gotta warn you, something like this—they're going to be on you like sharks to chum."

"That don't concern me, Angelo. You're a Christian, I'm a Muslim. You're a trainer and I'm a boxer. Life goes on."

"Life goes on, all right. It's just going to get hot is all I'm sayin'. And I'm not just talking about those guys out there. The whole world knows who the heavyweight champ is, especially a champ as mouthy as you. People are going to be upset."

"And I told you, that don't concern me. I can handle whatever they put on me, don't you worry. You train me and I'll fight. Simple as that."

"Simple as that," Angelo echoed, truly nervous about what the future held. Racial tensions were bad enough at the time, and now this.

A few weeks later, Cassius X became Muhammad Ali. Muhammad means "worthy of praise" and Ali means "most high." As Angelo predicted, all kinds of refuse hit the fan. Criticizers and detractors came at Ali from every direction. In Angelo's heart, he felt the treatment was totally unfair.

One morning at breakfast, Angelo opened the newspaper to read the headline "Black Muslims Take Over Boxing." He read the article aloud to Helen. Shockingly, the piece placed Muslims higher on the atrocity ladder than Nazis. He stopped reading when the children entered the room. Terri, who never missed a beat, caught that her father was upset about something.

"What's wrong, Daddy?"

"Nothing, sweetie, I just read a silly article," he said, pulling her onto his lap. "Did you have a good sleep? Did you dream about horses or unicorns?"

"No, no dreams. Can I please have cereal?"

Helen rose and mussed her daughter's hair as Jimmy came tearing into the kitchen with his fire truck in tow. He slid on the linoleum floor in his black socks and kept on sliding right into his father's leg. He laughed as Angelo pretended to be hurt.

"When's Mister Ali coming over again?"

"Soon, Jimmy. Soon."

"Why did he change his name again?"

Angelo looked at Helen, who gave a "you take this one" look.

"Well, son, he changed his name because of his religion."

"His religion is different from ours?" Jimmy looked worried.

"Yes, but both religions share all of the positive stuff, like the good stuff. For example, both religions believe that you should be good to others. The differences are really pretty small."

Jimmy's face seemed to relax. The phone rang.

"I'll get it," Angelo said, happy for the interruption. He picked up the receiver and said hello, then listened.

"Uh huh. Pardon me?" The pleasant expression on his face faded into storm clouds. "Listen to me, pal, the Dundees don't take kindly to that sort of talk." He slammed the receiver down.

"Who was that?" Helen asked.

"Some racist newspaper man."

"What's racist?" Jimmy asked.

Good grief.

"That's not the first call of that nature," Helen said quietly.

"What? Really?"

"I didn't want to upset you but I have a pretty good idea what the man just said to you. I've received a couple of calls too."

Angelo was furious. His family was off limits. Nobody had the right to bring this vile nonsense to his door.

"Is everything okay, Daddy?" Terri asked.

"Everything's fine, babe," he said, turning attention to Helen. "We might have to change our number and maybe go unlisted. Only let family and friends have the number."

"Let me know when you want to do it and I'll arrange it with the phone company."

"Sorry to bring this into our home, honey."

"You didn't bring anything, now let's enjoy our cereal," Helen said with wide eyes, indicating she didn't want to have the conversation in front of the children.

At the office, Angelo dove into work alongside Chris, making arrangements for a new fight, and hoping to put the morning unpleasantness behind him.

"Okay . . . same venue in Havana . . . three weeks sounds good . . . bye-bye."

Chris waited patiently for the phone call to end.

"So, the Ruiz fight is set, then?" Chris asked.

"All set. What's up?"

"Quite the circus you and Ali have going on. Have you read the papers?"

"Unfortunately."

"You were quoted in the *Journal*."

"How bad is it?"

"Not bad." Chris passed the paper to Angelo. "Here."

Angelo speed-read it until he found the quote.

"*. . . if those are the man's beliefs I have no problem with that.*"

He breathed a sigh of relief. "At least they didn't misquote me."

"Pop would agree, ya know, your stance on all this, standing by your guy." Chris said.

Angelo didn't respond.

"You catching any other heat?"

"Plenty."

"You hang in there. If you need anything—"

Chris let the words hang in the air, then returned to his desk and hopped on the phone. Angelo thanked him, but was unsure if Chris actually heard. It would take time and practice to become completely comfortable with the media.

While Muhammad was off on holiday, Angelo took the time to give extra attention to his other fighters. Willie Pastrano was nearing the end of his career but still had some fight left. Born in New Orleans, Pastrano came by his party lifestyle honestly, and Angelo had to work hard to keep him on point. At the best of times, Willie didn't like to train. Now it was even harder as his body aged.

Angelo let his mind drift back to the beginning when he and this tough Italian fighter were holed up in a hotel room in Louisville before a fight. Pastrano wasn't a big guy and struggled to stay heavy enough to hold weight. In those early days Angelo believed in a hefty amount of milk in the diet if a guy wanted to keep the weight on. Therefore, Pastrano could always be seen drinking milk. That was until Angelo noticed something screwy in Willie's behavior in the hotel room and took a sip from his milk bottle. The milk had a funny whisky taste to it.

"What the hell, Pastrano? You're in training."

"Whisky helps the milk go down, whadda ya want from me?" Willie replied.

As each fight date approached, Angelo stayed on Willie like glue, and not just because of the whisky and milk. Willie was a good-looking guy who was a hit with the ladies, even though he was married. Angelo was of the old school that a woman drained a fighter's energy if they partook in the pleasures before a fight. But more than that, it was the *pursuit* of women where most guys got into trouble. So, if babysitting was part of the trainer's job, Angelo did it.

With Pastrano slugging the bags, Angelo had to admit that his stable of Cuban fighters was also showing great results. It was as if Clay/Ali's victory energized all of the boxers at 5th Street Gym. Attention was pouring in from boxers, promoters, managers, and the press.

A rematch with Sonny Liston was scheduled for Ali. Angelo had no doubt he could beat the former champion yet again. That was, until he caught sight of *his* champ after vacation. Ali had piled on the pounds.

"Son of gun, what have you done? Were you hitting the buffet on an hourly basis?"

"It's just a coupla pounds, you ain't got to worry about me. I'm still the greatest," Muhammad Ali said, while shaking hands with some of the other fighters in the gym. Once the congratulations subsided, Angelo pulled Ali aside.

"Here's the straight skinny. You're puffed up and bloated. If you lose this rematch it will be because you beat yourself. It's gonna take some doin' to get you back dancing and floating again."

"All right, all right, don't make a big production out of all this."

The two men glared at each other. A smile slowly grew on Ali's face. They both laughed and hugged.

"When your name was Clay it was easier for me to help you with your little rhymes. What the heck am I going to rhyme with Ali?" Angelo laughed.

"*One, two, three, look and see, Liston put to sleep by Muhammad Ali,*" Ali trilled in a singsong voice.

"Nobody's knocking Liston out with that belly. Now, strap on your boots and go put five miles under those soles."

Muhammad grabbed Angelo in headlock and fake punched him rapidly in the head.

In a Howard Cosell impression Ali shouted, "Look at this! The champ has lost his mind and he's beating the stuffing out of his trainer. Somebody call security. Call the cops, call somebody, anybody!"

The other fighters howled at the spectacle before Ali let go.

Angelo righted himself. "Ya smudged up my glasses, ya big

dummy. Now, get out there and run before I throw you out on your ear!"

At the door Ali called, "You better be ready to train me when I get back. You'll be training a champion this time. It's gonna be different, Angelo."

"Get going and take that big belly with you!"

They worked extremely hard over the next few weeks. Angelo had to give the fighter credit; he put in the work and dropped the weight. The rematch was short. It happened so quickly that some called the finishing blow a "phantom punch." Once again, Ali found himself in the middle of controversy, as many accused the Ali camp of fixing the fight. Controversy had its downside and Ali began to lose popularity. First it was the religious affiliation, and now a suspect fight. Floyd Patterson stepped up and challenged Ali, claiming he was going to bring the belt back to America. Fans ate it up.

Angelo stood beside Ali as he boasted, "I'm gonna whoop Floyd and convert him from Christian to Muslim!" The reporters went ballistic.

Angelo leaned in and whispered, "Great job, champ. Now you've put us in the middle of a holy war. I wish you'd run this stuff by me first." Angelo would have much preferred to be low-key—an impossible task around Ali. He attempted to keep his head down and focus on his work, an attitude he adopted from his father. Anytime reporters tried to corner him, Angelo gave concise answers that reporters found unsatisfying. "My job is to get the champ ready for all comers."

"Hey, Ang," a reporter in a fedora and pencil-thin mustache called out, "is it true the boxing federation is going to strip Clay's belt?"

"I have heard no such thing, and for the record, his name is

Ali. You'd think a reporter would have done his homework on the champ's name."

The retort got laughs from the other reporters. The truth was, rumors had been floating around that the WBC was considering stripping Ali of his strap. Before they could badger him further, Angelo excused himself and went home. That evening the phone rang. It was Muhammad.

"Hiya, champ, what's the rumpus?"

"The Man wants me."

"Oh no, which branch?"

"Armed Forces."

"You got to be kidding me. They're throwing everything at ya, kid."

"I got no problem with no Viet Cong. I won't go. Not pointin' no gun at those people. I won't do it."

"Since when have they done this to a current belt holder? This is ridiculous. It's about the color of your skin."

"And because I'm Muslim."

Angelo knew the champ's words were true. How long could racial tension and religious insecurity go on in this country, he wondered?

"Celebrities' and politicians' kids get deferments all the time. This is injustice."

Muhammad agreed in a low tone. Silence filled the line.

"They're going to make life tough for you too. They might try and mess with your license. You've always been there for me, but you can stop now if you like. Your family doesn't need this."

"What they're doing is bullying, and I was raised to stand up to bullies. Nope, I'm in your corner," Angelo paused. "Literally."

"Thank you. How're Helen and the kids?"

"Great. They really want to see you."

"I bet Helen wants to see me the most," Ali said with a weak laugh.

"I changed my mind, you're on your own," Angelo laughed uncomfortably.

A week later, the boxing commission had the reason they were looking for to strip Ali of his title. Uncle Sam had called and Ali refused to go to war. As the Dundee family watched their fighter and friend on the television, they heard a familiar phrase.

"I ain't got no quarrel with them Viet Cong." Ali said it straight and clear.

"That's it, Helen," Angelo said. "He's a conscientious objector. They're going to arrest him. What a shame. Nine title defenses, then he's forced into exile."

"Oh, sweetie, this is horrible," Helen said, hugging him. They continued to watch the news.

"Does this mean jail?"

"Not right away. He's going to appeal."

"Which could take years!"

"He's my friend and he's a good man, Helen. He's in his prime, for heaven's sake. Those short-sighted, small-minded—"

The words caught in his throat as his eyes watered. Helen hugged him harder and cried along with him.

Chapter Six

MUHAMMAD ALI'S LONG ROAD BACK

While Ali spent four long years in exile from his profession, Angelo focused on his remaining fighters. He missed his friend, who had become like an adopted son. Even so, Angelo was busier than ever as he picked up a few guys along the way.

One day, the gym doors opened wide and in walked Muhammad Ali.

"The champ is back!" Ali shouted. "Did any of you suckas miss me?"

A round of applause filled the gym. Hugs, handshakes, and back-patting went all around. Although some in the public eye were not fond of the man, each and every fighter in the gym loved him. Boxers ignored the media hype for the most part. Fighters are a tough breed, and they felt for Ali. They could relate to a guy who had fought his way up to put food on the table, only to have it removed by the Man.

Angelo assessed the work before him. A layoff of three years or more would be suicide for many boxers because of "ring rust," the phenomenon of a boxer losing his step, timing, and precision. Any dip in the confidence department meant all bets were off; he'd be dinner for the other guy.

The current champ was Joe Frazier, the stocky, pound-for-pound heaviest hitter in the game. Ali claimed to want him immediately. Angelo could understand this, but was totally opposed. Luckily, he had an out.

"We've spoken to Frazier's camp. They want us to prove that you're ready to fight Frazier."

"That's them suckas just duckin' me."

"Muhammad," Angelo whispered. "I think it's a blessing in disguise. You've been off a long time. You need a tune-up fight."

"Aw, man," Ali said, waving the words off. Angelo could see that he agreed, but that he just needed to play the tough guy.

"Either way, there's no gettin' around it. It's the only way you get the shot. Ya gotta go through Jerry Quarry."

"That bum? He ain't no match for me."

Angelo stepped close and looked up to his fighter. "Then lay him flat on the canvas and we'll get closer to the belt."

"*My* belt."

"Your belt."

As the weeks went by, Angelo was pleased with Ali's conditioning. However, during sparring it was clear that he wasn't as sharp as he was prior to the layoff. Despite Angelo's fears, the fight with Quarry went according to plan with Ali winning by TKO in the third round of the October 26, 1970, fight. Had Ali been up against Joe Frazier that night, he'd have lost the fight. Still, it was a nice confidence booster.

"Next up, we've got Oscar Bonavena. Now listen, champ, this won't be no Jerry Quarry. This guy knocked Frazier down twice; he ain't no *pomodoro puo*."

"How many times I tell you about that funny language of yours? What's that mean?"

Angelo laughed. "It means he ain't no tomato can."

That evening, as Angelo drove home from the gym, he was exhausted. He grinned thinking of Ali fast-talking his way into Carmen Basilio's hotel room those many years ago. How he'd talked their ears off! Angelo and Ali had been through wars together, and at some point the relationship evolved from boxer and trainer to friends—good friends. The added emotional component made Angelo want to protect his fighter more than ever before. It was even more reason to take the Bonavena fight more seriously.

The work hours were logged. Finally, it was fight night— December 7, 1970. As Ali and crew made their way to the ring, Angelo couldn't recall an arena that had ever been this loud. Madison Square Garden was on fire. He could only imagine how his fighter felt at hearing the ear-splitting chant, "Ali, Ali, Ali!"

The comeback kid stepped into the ring wearing a red robe with white letters. He tested the canvas with his usual fancy footwork movements. As the referee went over the rules, Ali taunted his opponent, as was his custom from the old days. The bell rang and the two men went at it. Ali was by far the more skilled boxer, but Bonavena was renowned for his heavy hands. From his corner, Angelo watched intently. To his eye, Ali was still not crisp, not like he once was. Still, the trainer made sure not to over-coach between rounds.

He knew Ali's rhythm was lying just beneath the surface and that Ali would find it. With some fighters, especially one of this caliber, sometimes it was better to stay out of the way.

The rounds ticked away with Ali in the lead. Not a

comfortable lead, however. A hard left hook seriously rocked him and set his legs wobbling. He was in trouble.

"That's it, be tough in there," Angelo called. "Hands up, now."

With masterful head movements followed by stand-up grappling, Ali held on.

"You're looking good, champ," Angelo shouted as Ali seated himself heavily on the stool, heaving for breath.

"Watch out for his left hook. He starts it low like an upper-cut then rotates it into a hook. Be ready, I don't want you rocked again. Now, go get 'im, champ."

Ali moved toward his opponent. Like magic, his rhythm returned. He went after Bonavena with added heat to his combinations.

"That's what I call a second wind," he shouted at his corner-men. Jaws dropped all around.

The two fighters traded all the way to the fifteenth and final round. Ali got caught with another left hook but it had no heat to it. A few minutes in, Ali pulled the same move Bonavena had been attempting all evening. He leaped forward, slightly stiff-legged, and landed a short, hard left-right to Bonavena's jaw. The man went down to the canvas for the first time in his career. Then, he regained his feet.

"Give him a standing eight count, ref!" Angelo yelled.

But the ref did not comply. Bonavena lunged for Ali. They mixed it up briefly before Ali connected again, knocking the South American boxer down a second time. Angelo checked the time; just over a minute left. His heart raced with hope that Ali could continue.

"Go get him! He's yours!"

Ali threw a final combination at the staggering Bonavena

and put him on the canvas a third time. Ali threw his hands in the air. The crew leaped into the ring. Television viewers all over the world heard boxing announcer Howard Cosell shout, "It's all over! It's all over!"

Chapter Seven

ALI-FRAZIER AND THE FATE OF THE GREATEST

Helen carried a plate of seasoned T-bone steaks out onto the porch, where Angelo was working the barbecue. She wore her hair in a loose ponytail and was dressed in casual clothes for a day of relaxation. Angelo gave her a quick kiss as he scooted coals around the cooker. Muhammad, decked out in a blue and white short-sleeve button-up shirt, was playing with the kids. He dropped to one knee, holding his hands up for little Jimmy to box. Every now and then Ali would move his hands away, causing Jimmy to swing at air.

"Angelo, haven't you taught this boy anything? He's slower than a slug moving uphill in a snowstorm."

"*You're* slower than a slug, Mr. Ali," Jimmy said, pointing a tiny finger at Ali, who made a face like he was in shock.

"Me, slower than a slug? Ha, I once had a cheetah ask me how come I'm so fast!"

"No way," Jimmy said, laughing hysterically.

Ali got to his feet. "Helen, before you go inside, would you please tell your husband that not only am I the greatest fighter but I'm also the greatest griller?"

"That may be true, but nobody touches that grill but the man of the house."

"Daddy's grill," Terri said, in support of her father. "I bet you can't even cook. You're too busy running your mouth."

Helen held out an apron for her husband.

"I won't be needing that, honey," he replied.

"Oh, really? And who's going to launder that shirt when it's covered in grease and barbecue sauce?" she asked, moving her hands to her hips.

"There won't be a speck on it, I promise."

"After all these years of marriage," Ali said. "You still don't know when a woman's got you beat?" He turned to Helen. "Are you sure being married to Angelo isn't a condition of your parole?"

"Don't start that racket," Angelo warned, pointing a barbecue fork.

"I'm waiting," Helen said, holding the apron with an outstretched hand. Angelo hemmed and hawed until he finally took the apron and put it on. Ali practically leaped in the air when he saw the inscription on the front.

"Aw no, uh-uh, no way. Helen, he can't wear that. He's too ugly. Only someone as pretty as you or me can wear that."

The apron had the words *Kiss the Cook* on the front.

"Come on, Helen . . . must I? He'll be ribbing me all night, you know how he is."

"You'll survive, sweetie," she said, retreating to the kitchen.

Angelo faced Ali with a crestfallen look. "Okay, let's have it."

"Just because you got that flirtatious apron on don't mean you're pretty. Don't be gettin' no crazy ideas now."

"Good, you've had your joke. Now, knock it off for five seconds while we talk shop." Angelo peeked under one of the sizzling T-bones.

"Shoot."

"How ya holding up? Bonavena hit you with some big shots."

"What? Have you got amnesia or something? Don't you remember how it ended?"

"Of course I do. But we need you a hundred percent for Frazier."

Ali cocked his head to the side and made sleepy eyes in response.

"Don't give me that look either. You know we trainers hear things and this guy's been busting ribs and cracking craniums."

"Maybe you trainers can hear, but you sure can't smell, otherwise you'd know you burnin' them steaks."

"I'm doing no such—oh no!" Angelo turned a juicy T-bone, causing a huge flame to escape in the air. He jumped back, barely avoiding singeing his eyebrows.

"Helen," Ali called, "Julia Child is out here burning these steaks."

Angelo quickly moved the remaining beef to a cooler part of the grill. Ali doubled over with laughter just as Helen and the kids came running out. The children started laughing too and Helen giggled behind her hand.

"That's it, laugh it up," said Angelo. "I hope you appreciated my quick footwork in avoiding the fire. Take notes, everybody, take notes."

Prepping for the Frazier fight took weeks of nonstop work inside the ropes. Outside the ropes, Ali ran his mouth at mach speed to the delight and outrage of sportswriters and fans. Angelo combined the information he'd gathered from tapes of Frazier and the lessons learned from the Bonavena fight. Ali could not afford to make a single mistake because Joe Frazier was a one-man wrecking ball. In truth, Angelo was a bit nervous about the fight. His fighter was back, but he didn't seem to be all the way back. Additionally, Ali's pre-fight taunting only seemed to enrage Joe Frazier. The taunting had worked with most guys but Angelo feared this might be a poke-the-sleeping-tiger situation.

The fear had some basis. From round one Ali was on the balls of his feet, peppering away at the head of Joe Frazier. But Frazier moved into the shots and even smiled at times. Angelo didn't like it one bit.

Ali's combinations looked crisp to Angelo, and would have frustrated lesser men, but Frazier took the shots and kept on coming. Up close, it was easy to see just how dangerous Frazier's left hook was. Ali took several blows to the head, but in his typical fashion shook his head as if to say "No, that wasn't nothin'" for the crowd.

At the end of round four, Ali joined Angelo at the stool.

"Listen, kid, you've got to respect that left hook. He bobs low then comes up from both feet and launches it high. D'ya hear me? He always starts low and leaps with it. He's catching you with it. Don't let 'im. Okay?"

Ali's chest heaved up and down as he replied, "He ain't nuthin'. I got this chump. He ain't nuthin'."

The next few rounds ticked by. The fight was close and that was not good for a challenger. To beat a champion the win had to be definitive, otherwise the belt holder kept his strap.

While Ali's conditioning couldn't be faulted, his combinations began to lose some of their pep, and Frazier's left hook kept tagging. A lot of guys would have been stretched out by this time. But Ali was built tough, which was a comforting thought to Angelo, but no trainer wanted to see his fighter take shot after shot to the jaw.

"That's it, Ali, tie him up if you need to! Then move away from that darn hook! Let's go!"

Ali sat down heavily after the eighth. The corner guys gave him water and put an ice pack at the back of his neck. Ali spat excess water into the bucket.

Angelo leaned low over the stool. "Keep that right hand up," he said to Ali. "He's coming over the top with that hook. Right before he throws it, his hands are open. Time it right and take his block off, okay? Use your speed, son, use your speed."

"Okay, Ang."

Ali got to his feet seconds before the bell.

"And please, please keep that right up. We can't keep taking that hook all night. Please!"

The dancer returned in the ninth. Ali, on the balls of his feet, appeared rejuvenated. He danced in and out, tagging Frazier with lightning-quick jabs. Angelo's heart rate accelerated. Could it be that his guy was back? Ali threw a sweet one-two combination, then hung on. The ref separated the fighters. Ali kept up the pressure to win the round.

Round ten came and went. Dundee's excitement began to subside as the adrenaline burst that had fueled the ninth round vanished. Frazier began working Ali's body. Angelo flinched with nearly every shot.

By the fourteenth, Ali had another short burst of energy and speed until Frazier loaded up a left hook from Thursday of the previous week. He literally left the canvas, leaping forward from both tree-trunk thighs and caught Ali square "on the button," as insiders call it, also known as "taking it on the chin." Angelo watched his friend and fighter hit the canvas for just the third time in his career.

An exhausted Muhammad Ali told Dundee, "The greatest is gone."

Back in the dressing room, Angelo removed Muhammad's hand wraps, speaking in a low voice to his sullen, battered boxer. Even though the fight was over, crowd noise from the famous Madison Square Garden continued to seep into the dressing room. The other members of the team were quiet with the occasional "You'll be back, champ" and "We'll get him next time."

Angelo chose his words carefully. "We both know that when we get knocked down in this business, we get back up. Now, I know it sounds cliché but it's a fact. You cannot let this loss get you down. After Doc Ferdie gives you the all-clear, you rest a few days, then we'll get right back at it."

Ali nodded, not taking his eyes off the hand wraps.

"It's not going to be an easy road back because Frazier's not going to give you a fight right away," Angelo continued. "They want you to fight a couple of the other top ten guys."

"He's protecting his belt," Ali mumbled.

"He's protecting his belt, I agree. That fight was too close. Joe knows it and his camp knows it and most important," Angelo paused, forcing Ali to look at him, "*we* know it."

Ali nodded three times slowly, then mumbled, "Yeah."

"We have the advantage here, Ali, don't think we don't. We'll use these other fights to sharpen you up, get your accuracy back. Then we'll take the fight to Frazier, because now," Angelo smiled, "we know what he's got."

Ali grinned. "I think you're crazy, Dundee. Maybe even crazier than me."

"There's my guy," Angelo said, patting his back in a half hug.

"Now get cleaned up, cleared by the doc, and I'll see ya in a couple days."

"Sure thing, Ang."

Chapter Eight

LIKE FATHER, LIKE SON

Ever since Jimmy was a child, he occasionally got to go with his father to work. The boxers always made a big deal out of his kids. When little Jimmy tried on a pair of oversized gloves, he looked ridiculous, and Angelo got a big kick out it. Being around fighters seemed to pique Jimmy's interest. He asked a thousand questions a minute. What do the hand wraps do? How much water do you give the fighter between rounds? Does blood hurt? Angelo joyfully fielded every one.

At first, Helen wasn't enthused about their son hanging around the gym, but over time she grew into the idea. She understood the joy it brought her husband to spend time with their son, and that Jimmy was taking an interest in his dad's profession.

If Jimmy had wanted to become a boxer, Angelo would have hell to pay, or rather, Helen to pay. But as he grew, Jimmy seemed to want to work the corner just like his pop.

Angelo attempted to find the right balance between steady

guidance and allowing Jimmy to make his own way. The boy worked hard and paid attention. The guys seemed to take a liking to him. Angelo could not have been more proud, especially on the day Jimmy informed him that he'd been asked to corner as cut man at a local fight.

"This is a big deal, son. I'm proud o' ya."

"Thanks, Pop, I'm pretty proud myself. A little nervous, though."

"You wouldn't be human if you weren't," Angelo smiled.

Jimmy pulled out his lunchbox, peeled off a piece of bread, and put two pieces of capicola on it. He chased it down with a sip of soda.

"I have a favor to ask," he said. "I don't want you coming to my first fight, Pop. I'm too nervous."

"Aw, that stinks. Really? I've been fired up about this. Your debut match, are you sure your dear old dad can't—"

"Just not on this first one. Sorry, Dad."

"Well, if that's the way you want it—" Angelo said, letting the words hang.

"Just on this first one," Jimmy said, patting his dad's hand.

"Maybe I'm just being a sap. I'm proud o' ya, son. You're gonna do great." Angelo forced a smile. In truth, he was a bundle of pride and nerves. Maybe Jimmy was right and his son didn't need a mother hen looking over his shoulder. Still . . .

"Angelo Dundee, you hang up that jacket and put those car keys away," Helen said sternly.

"But, honey," Angelo pleaded, "I'm climbing the walls here."

"You think I haven't noticed? You're scurrying around like a cockroach searching for the exit."

"Helen, he's my boy."

"*Your* boy?"

"Our boy. Come on, Helen, I gotta go."

"But, sweetie, you told him you wouldn't. What if he sees you and blows it? He'd never forgive you."

Angelo stared at his wife with one arm inside his jacket sleeve and the other out, with car keys dangling from his hand.

"Babe, please."

"Look at you, you're all knotted up on this, aren't you?" Helen smiled sympathetically.

Angelo nodded, remaining in place.

"Here's the deal," she said, helping him on with sleeve number two. "You creep in the back way and you stay up in those bleachers, do you hear me? So Jimmy doesn't know you're there, not even afterward."

"Yes, I promise." Angelo tried not to grin too hard.

Helen reached into the closet. "Here, take your trilby. I don't want him seeing that beautiful bald head of yours."

"Helen, you are the greatest," he said, and kissed her.

"I know that, honey. Now go have fun and stay outta sight!"

Angelo timed it perfectly, and why not? He'd been in the game long enough to know the routine. The fight was going down at a local joint called Rory's, a good place for scouting new talent. He knew the security guards at the back of the hall and they let him in after some brief fight talk. His son, fighter, and crew were all in the dressing room getting ready. Angelo crept by unnoticed and climbed up to the fifth level of seats in the small gym.

The place was busy with raucous beer-drinking fight fans. Cigarette and cigar smoke added great cover, not that he thought his son would ever glance up to his row. A few familiar faces came by and he made them all promise not to mention his presence. A few fellas teased that he was hiding out from his wife, but they knew better.

Jimmy was cornering for a southpaw named "Stevie Boy" Simms. The fighter was tough but it would be no easy night for him. His opponent, "Mad Dog" Mike Seavers, was a brawler with heavy hands. Stevie Boy's trainer was in the house, a man by the name of Cole Pritchard. Angelo knew and respected him. If he spotted Angelo, would he tell his fighter, who might leak to the other guys in the corner? Maybe this was all a big mistake. The butterflies in Angelo's belly were driving him crazy.

The first four rounds were too close to call—the judges could have called it either way. Halfway through the fifth, Stevie Boy received a stiff shot to his right eye courtesy of Mad Dog's overhand left. Blood trickled down the side of his face. Jimmy would have to go to work between the rounds. *You're in the soup now, son . . .*

Thirty seconds remained. Angelo couldn't contain himself. He moved down the seats and pushed toward the ring. Cursing his short stature, he had to move up quite close to get a good look. Two rowdy fans, both over six feet tall, stood between him and Jimmy's corner. He stayed hidden while peeking around them at the ring.

Trainer Cole squeezed water into his fighter's mouth while giving instructions. Angelo could barely make out his words over the noise. Jimmy stood by Stevie Boy while the trainer spoke. Blood continued to drip down his fighter's face. Angelo cringed slightly but stayed put.

Another forty seconds passed before Jimmy moved in and worked the cut. He pressed a heavy amount of gauze directly on the wound and applied pressure. Next came a Q-tip, just as Angelo had taught him. Suddenly, one of the guys providing cover in front of Angelo jerked to one side. Angelo was left totally exposed, in plain sight of Jimmy.

"Dang it," he said, and ducked back behind the big man, unsure if he'd been seen.

The ref gave the "final seconds" warning. Stevie Boy stood up, ready to go. The bell sounded and the two combatants met center-ring. Angelo slunk back toward the bleachers. By the time he'd reached his seat, Stevie Boy was a bloody mess. Angelo didn't bother sitting; he moved back down the aisle toward the back exit.

He considered heading over to the Moon Landing Bar, where many of the fight fans and sportswriters hung out, but decided against it. He wasn't in the mood. Instead, he went home to Helen and told her what happened.

They were still up when Jimmy came home. The boy kissed his mother, then gave his father a frosty look.

He saw me, all right, Angelo said to himself.

"How was your first fight, honey?" Helen asked.

"Referee stoppage. Stevie Boy bled like a stuck pig and I couldn't stop it."

Angelo tried to look innocent.

"I suppose Dad has already told you? He was there."

Angelo shot Helen a look, then said, "Son, I'm sorry. I just couldn't stand it. Boxing has been my life and now you're in the game. Please try and see it my way."

"All I know is you broke your promise, Dad."

"I know and I'm sorry."

"Sorry doesn't cut it," Jimmy said, heading toward his bedroom.

"Wait a minute, son, we're not done yet. You don't walk away until the conversation is over, you know that."

Jimmy stopped, turned, and faced his father. "What?"

"I've apologized and I meant it. But now we need to talk shop and you need to listen."

Jimmy folded his arms across his chest and leaned against the refrigerator.

"I hate to say it, but Stevie Boy may have had a shot at staying in that fight."

"How do you figure?"

"When you see a cut, and you're the cut man, that is priority number one. No ifs, ands, or buts."

"But I had to let Cole do his job."

"You do your job while he's doing his. It's the only shot your fighter has. The trainer talks and you plug that leak. You've got to get that gauze on the cut with pressure the second your guy's butt hits that stool. Every time, all the time!"

Jimmy's eyes moved down to the floor. Angelo could tell his son was taking the words to heart. Helen's face remained impassive. She knew whose show this was.

"So you're saying I cost Stevie that fight? I feel horrible," Jimmy said, sitting dejectedly in a kitchen chair.

"I'm not saying you did and I'm not saying you didn't. Fights can go many ways. Your goal is to do your job to the best of your ability. If anybody looks back on it, you're in the clear. It's also how a guy builds a good reputation."

Jimmy pinched the bridge of his nose. "Should I apologize to Stevie Boy?"

"Up to you. As I said, many factors figure the outcome of a fight. One thing for sure is that you will learn from this and move forward."

Angelo moved to the fridge and pulled two beers from it. He sat down and handed one to Jimmy.

"Like I said, learn and move on. Don't be afraid to ask for help once in a while. I had all kinds of help coming up from your Uncle Chris, Chickie Ferrara, Dr. Pacheco, and tons of other guys."

Jimmy raised his bottle and took a sip.

"But you know who helped me more than anybody?"

"Who's that?"

"A fine filly who goes by the name Helen."

Helen came over and gently put a hand on her husband's shoulder. "Son, I want you to know that I did everything I could to stop your stubborn father."

Angelo laughed. "Oh, I get it, Helen. You're the good cop and I'm the bad cop. Thanks for nuthin'."

Helen joined the boys at the table. Angelo got up and poured his wife a glass of red.

"*Salute*," she said, raising her glass. The men clinked glasses.

Chapter Nine

TAKE THE BITTER WITH THE SWEET

While Muhammad Ali had been in boxing exile, Angelo continued his usual training with other fighters. One of those was Jimmy Ellis, a thirty-one-year-old born in Louisville, Kentucky, Ali's hometown. Working together while Ali was out of the picture, Angelo and Ellis racked up several victories. The boxing federation set up a tournament between eight fighters to see who would be the number-one contender to take on Joe Frazier. Ellis came out on top. Unfortunately, Ellis lost to Frazier in an attempt to unify the belts.

Then, Ali came back. He and Angelo resumed their training schedule. It was a grind at his age, but Ali stepped up and took on all comers. One of those comers was Jimmy Ellis. Now Angelo found himself in a position of conflict: he was not only Ellis's trainer, but he was also his manager. He was training and managing the challenger to Ali!

"I was afraid of this," Angelo admitted.

"What's that?" said Ali.

"It's like this—you're my friend and I'm your trainer. The same goes with Jimmy Ellis, but I'm also his manager. I'm kinda Ellis's whole team, not just part of his team like I am with you."

"I hear what you're saying. You gotta throw in with Jimmy."

"I gotta throw in with Jimmy, yes. I'm sorry."

"I understand," Muhammad said with a downturned head. After a moment of silence, a slight smile came to his face.

"But if you think for one second that you and Ellis can beat me because you know my tricks, and because he was my sparring partner, I got news for you suckas. It ain't gonna happen. Not now, not ever, not in any kind of weather."

"Is that right?" Angelo said, relieved at how easily Ali took the news.

"I've been holding back a few things of my own, a few things only someone this pretty could possibly know. And when I box, I box oh so well. And if you ain't sure, just ask Howard Cosell."

With that, Ali raised both hands in the air, proclaimed he was still the greatest, and danced out of the room. Angelo shook his head and smiled, thinking, *That kid never turns it off.*

During a press conference Ali claimed that he was done with Angelo Dundee, that they were through, regardless of the outcome.

"Really?" One of the reporters asked, "Even after everything the two of you have been through?"

"That's right, but let's say Angelo came crawling back. I'd only consider it if he stopped talking so much."

Some people took Ali at his word but it was all pre-fight hype. Ali confirmed as much with a quick wink to Angelo when the cameras were off at the end of the conference.

~

It was July 26, 1971, and Disney World had opened in Orlando, Florida. Richard M. Nixon was president of the United States and Charles Manson was given the death penalty earlier in the year. The fight was scheduled for the Houston Astrodome, where the Astros went seventy-nine and eight-three on the season. When fight night arrived, Angelo felt odd not being in Ali's corner. A true professional, he had coached Ellis as best he could, with every intention of winning the match. Ellis was no match for Ali, but he did make it to the twelfth round before the referee stopped the fight. Ellis earned a TKO on his record.

With the Ellis fight out of the way, Angelo and Ali reunited as a team and took on more opponents. Ali had racked up a few wins and his confidence was back—perhaps too much so. He stepped into a ring without taking Ken Norton seriously and paid the price. Norton put Ali against the ropes and pounded away. He pounded and pounded until he broke Ali's jaw.

Wincing, Angelo could only imagine the level of pain his fighter was feeling. Ali kept on fighting without complaint. He managed to battle partway back, but ultimately it wasn't enough. Ali lost in a split decision.

Would Ali bounce back from the Norton loss? Angelo was worried until he got a phone call from an ecstatic Ali.

"I'm shaking things up. You always come up with new ideas, at least you think you do. Now it's my turn."

"What have you got?"

"I've moved training camp to Deer Lake in Pennsylvania. It's a great five-acre outdoor space, great for running and hiking. I'm talkin' 'bout nature, Ang, you need more nature in your life. The city has made you soft. You're gonna love it."

"What's the pasta like out there?"

"I swear you got a one-track mind. Just get your butt out

here. We got work to do. I want my title back! Aaagh!" The line went dead.

A week later Angelo climbed into a car that had been sent to take him from the plane to Deer Lake. As it passed through the gate at the bottom of the lengthy gravel driveway, a large tin sign read: *Muhammad Ali Training Camp.*

"This must be the place," Angelo remarked.

The property was vast; it seemed to go on forever. The car wheeled up to a massive cabin structure with thick logs ending in finger joints. Muhammad stepped outside wearing chunky hiking boots, track pants, and a white T-shirt that exposed his muscled frame. A smile stretched ear to ear as he opened the car door for his trainer.

Angelo got out, saying, "This is absolutely beautiful. Picturesque."

"It's nice being away from all of that press and city noise. Come meet everybody."

Angelo looked around, admiring the giant trees that framed the cabin, then took a deep breath of the crisp, fresh air.

"Wow," he said, lifting his bag and heading into the huge log cabin–style gym. High ceilings were accented with grand arched windows. The ring was located right in the middle. Off to the left, a single heavy bag was suspended beneath a large skylight. Who wouldn't want to work a bag like that as the sun streaked across the leather? It was beautiful.

More than forty people were inside. Some were fight people Angelo recognized, as well as a few celebrities. The smell of sizzling beef met his nostrils. Searching for the source, he saw a large kitchen with a sign titled "10 Rules of the Kitchen." His favorite was number ten: *This kitchen belongs to the cook. If you don't believe it, try something!*

Weeks came and went. Some of the hangers-on regarded Angelo with what appeared to be suspicion, but then more like jealousy. Ali needed people around—he loved an audience. Some people craved his attention so much that it bordered on possessiveness. Angelo understood this to a certain degree because Ali's charm and enthusiasm were so infectious, but he would not let anything interfere with their work. Calling on the work ethic passed down from his father, Angelo ignored the gossip and jeers, kept his head down, and focused on his fighter. The Norton rematch was around the corner—there was no time for petty games.

Ali's new cardio regimen was going well, in addition to which he hiked and chopped wood. Angelo had no doubt that Muhammad could beat Ken Norton in a rematch.

Aside from the few petty hangers-on, Ali had gathered a family of sorts around himself. They ate meals together, during which the conversation was always upbeat. It reminded Angelo of childhood—he embraced it.

When the time came to meet, Ali adopted a new mantra. Throughout training he called out to all within earshot, "Nobody beats me twice." It was so often repeated that the entire camp believed the words. Even before the fight, in the dressing room he chanted, "Nobody beats me twice, nobody!" In the ring, his mantra held. Ali was more fit than the first meeting of the two fighters, and to show his stamina he chose to stand between rounds instead of sitting on the stool. Angelo thought the tactic, although small, would have some psychological effect on Norton. In the middle rounds Ali was forced into a defensive posture as Norton pressed forward and pushed Ali back.

"Don't let him fight his fight, Ali," Angelo said to him. "He likes pushing guys around. Move laterally and use that jab of yours."

Ali nodded and jumped back in the fight. He finished with a string of flurries.

"There he goes," Angelo shouted. "I think he just edged Norton out, boys."

When the dust settled and the exhausted warriors gulped water and toweled off, the decision came down. Ali won by split decision.

The time had come to avenge the loss to "Smokin' Joe" Frazier. Since they'd last jousted, Frazier had defended his title ten times. That was before running into George Foreman—he took Frazier out at 1:35 of the second round. Ali wanted a shot at the title but knew he had to beat Frazier first to do it.

After a great sparring session, Angelo helped Ali remove his headgear and squirted some water into his mouth.

"That's good for today. We thought you'd be fighting Joe for the belt, but now it looks like he's the stepping-stone to the belt. How do you feel about that?" Angelo asked.

"Do you remember when Joe Louis said, 'He can run, but he can't hide'?"

When Angelo heard that question, he knew to listen carefully. Ali was not only a highly skilled fighter, he was one of the smartest boxers he'd ever trained. He knew the hours Ali put into strategy, and that he'd studied Frazier inside and out.

"That belt can run but it can't hide. When I find it, it's staying around *my* waist, nobody else's. I'm fine fightin' Frazier. I need to prove that if you beat me once it's 'cause you got lucky, and we all know luck runs out. I'm takin' out Joe, then I'm on to George."

"That's what I like to hear."

"What else?"

"Just remember Frazier took out Ellis in four rounds and it took you longer than that."

Muhammad tilted his head sideways and made sleepy eyes at his trainer. Angelo leaned against the ropes.

"I know I'm comparing apples and oranges here but—" he let it trail off.

"Was it tough, Ang, having to throw in the towel like that for your fighter?"

"It was tougher seeing Frazier nearly kill my guy in the ring. Yeah, it was tough, but I'll always protect my fighter. I hope you know that."

"Sure I do. I didn't hire you for your pretty face."

The two men remained silent as Angelo unwrapped the fighter's hands. There were many times when the two were silent, more than other people knew.

Finally, Ali said, "You're worried about me gettin' hurt and you shouldn't do that, Ang. I'm the best this game's ever seen and before you and I are done they'll say you were the best trainer they've ever seen too. So you train and I'll box and we'll win. Deal?"

"Deal."

With the wraps off, Ali massaged his hands a moment and turned to leave the ring.

"Hang on a second, champ. How bad are they?"

"What you talkin' 'bout, Dundee?"

"Your hands, how are they? They're the most precious tools a fighter's got and I know yours have been bugging you. I've been at this too long not to notice."

"Man, I'm tellin' you, as fast and powerful as these suckas are, they're causing this brother some serious grief. They hurt nonstop, whether I'm in the ring or out. I've been soaking them, icing them, massaging them in some special Chinese balm. Ain't nothin' workin'."

"Son of a gun."

"What about surgery? What you think?"

Angelo exhaled deeply. "You want my honest answer?"

"It's why I'm askin' you."

"I've heard it works for some guys."

"And the other guys?"

"I had a guy get it done back in '68—it ruined him mentally. He was so freaked out about breaking his hands. His giant left hook was so reduced in power, he couldn't break tissue paper. And that's not the only guy that's happened to."

"I've heard those stories too. I just wanted to see what you heard."

"Let me talk to Ferdie Pacheco and see what he thinks. We'll get ya fixed up one way or another."

"Doc Ferdie's one of the best."

"He is at that."

"I knock fools out with these hands 'cause I'm the greatest fighter of these lands."

"Not your best rhyme, I'm afraid."

"What? With these hands I take suckas out. With these hands I win all the bouts!"

"*All* the bouts, Ali?"

"Look, you're obviously tired 'cause I worked you too hard.

It's affecting your hearing." He laughed. "Go home, Dundee. Meanwhile, I'm gonna walk the streets and look pretty."

On the drive home, thoughts of his fighter's hands continued to haunt Angelo. He'd put a little extra confidence in his words to Ali, as far as what Doc Ferdie Pacheco could do, because he didn't want Ali to worry. But in all honesty, he *was* worried. Very few fighters were the same after hand surgery. There were confidence issues, numbing, tingling sensations, random shooting pains, and more.

Doc Pacheco divided his time between Miami and New York, and right now he was in town. He'd call him when he got home. Up to this point, Angelo had never heard of a solution outside of surgery, but that didn't mean there wasn't a cure. If there was anything to be done, Angelo was going to find it.

After Helen's delectable chicken parmigiana with mashed potatoes and lemon-flavored green beans, Angelo got Doc Ferdie Pacheco on the phone.

"What's up, Doc?" Angelo asked in his best Bugs Bunny impression.

"Don't you get tired of that crap, Dundee?" Ferdie Pacheco answered.

"Not a chance. I suppose you know why I'm calling, because if I've noticed, you've noticed too—"

"Muhammad's hands."

"Yes, Muhammad's hands. We talked about surgery today."

"You know what happens there," Ferdie said.

"Mentally, you mean."

"Yes. In this sport it's all about mind and body."

"Yeah, don't I know it? What do you suggest?"

"I've got to have a look, of course, but there's some pretty impressive balms on the market nowadays."

"He's tried those."

"We don't know what he's tried unless he told you."

"Good point, Doc. Anything else?"

"As you know, men weren't meant to pound on other men's craniums, Dundee. Hands aren't built for that."

"As enlightening as that is, Doc, can we move it along?"

"I'd have thought life in the sunshine would make you more patient, not less. Maybe you ought to move back to the Big Apple."

"Wow, getting a straight answer out of you is like trying to read Cantonese," Angelo chuckled. It felt good talking with his old friend.

"I'm just trying to put the patient at ease. It's called bedside manner."

"I only need Helen at my bedside, thank you very much. Now can we—"

"Might be more fun if she was actually in the bed. Anyway, the news isn't good, depending on the severity of his hands. But if he can still fight, what some guys do is inject a little cocktail of cortisone and some other vitamins into the hands and then when the career is over," he said, "get the surgery. Naturally, I'll have to check him out myself."

"That's the best you scientists have come up with?"

"The hands are delicate, my friend. I didn't invent the sport of bashing on human skulls and bags filled with sand."

"I know, I know," Angelo said rubbing a hand over his head. "I just wish there was something else. What you're saying is, 'Do like football players do.' Shoot yourself up, feel no pain, but the damage is done, right?"

"I've been reading some interesting articles on Chinese acupuncture, but I'm still doing the research on that."

Angelo figured the hands talk was exhausted for the time being.

"How are the paintings coming along, Ferd?" Angelo asked, picturing his longtime friend standing in his living room surrounded by artwork.

"I'm still an amateur but getting better every day. You should try it sometime."

"I'm all thumbs when it comes to art, I'm afraid. But get me on a dance floor and look out."

"That's good. You need a side passion to survive this wacky game."

"I think you might be right on that, Ferd."

For the second fight with Frazier on January 28, 1974, Ali did his usual pre-fight hype. Reporters ate it up. Set for a return to Madison Square Garden, boxing enthusiasts termed it "Super Fight II." Ali would be avenging a loss, and he made it clear he was very charged up for the bout. Everybody was happy that his intense passion had returned.

On fight night, Frazier threw his famed left hooks but Ali dodged or deflected most of them. It was a frustrating night for Frazier. Ali was the victor by unanimous decision. In Angelo's opinion, that made Ali one of the greatest, if not *the* greatest: He lost, studied, prepared, then returned and vanquished. If Super Fight II hadn't lived up to the hype, it didn't matter that the fight wasn't a barnburner of a brawl. At the end, Ali's hand was raised in the air and that was all that mattered. He had proven once again that "the Greatest" never lost to the same guy twice.

They were now set for another shot at the title. Beating Joe Frazier had clinched it.

∼

Eight months later, Angelo was up at night with insomnia. The upcoming George Foreman fight weighed heavily on his mind. He was truly scared. George was, pound for pound, the heaviest hitter Angelo had ever seen. He had a string of knockouts—not just a few—a string! Sure, Ali was the better boxer, but Foreman was dropping guys with body shots. Heck, he was dropping guys with his set-up punches. He had knocked Frazier down three times, for Pete's sake! Ali was tough, but who can survive a sledgehammer to the rib cage?

The next morning, Angelo got to the gym early to go over things with Ali—a pep talk and strategy. The strategy would be simple—don't get hit by that Goliath! Eventually, other fighters strolled in.

Ali arrived after his six-mile jog. Angelo marveled briefly at his heavy combat boots, an accessory to his running regimen. As Angelo began to express what was on his mind, Ali cut him off, as was often his custom.

"I'm thinking of calling this one the 'Rumble in the Jungle' because when these two brothers hit that jungle, boy, we gonna rumble. We gonna rumble in the jungle! What do you think? I came up with it last night."

"I like it," Angelo smiled. "But while you were working your poetry I was up half the night trying to figure out a way through this guy. You've seen his fights, right?"

"Yeah, I've seen his fights. I saw what he did to Joe, but Joe was too slow and George is even slower. I'm gonna dance to that big oak tree and chop it down. So you can wipe that scared look of your face. And that goes for everyone else around here."

Ali stepped into the middle of the ring in his clunky workmen's boots and sweat-soaked tracksuit.

"I see your sad faces. You think Ali's goin' down. Uh-huh, suckas, that big tree is too slow. He's like a big bear tryin' to swat a fly. And when we get to Zaire it's Ali's name you're gonna hear!"

Ali did an impression of George's giant telegraphed haymakers and growled like a grizzly.

"I could dodge those punches in my sleep. I'm gonna float like a butterfly and sting like a bee. Poor George won't even see me until he wakes up and sees the belt around my waist."

Ali capped it all off with a quick flurry, then his patented shuffle. The other fighters clapped and cheered. Angelo took the speech he'd had chambered in his head and threw it away.

"Well," he said, leaning toward his cut man, "he's not lacking in the confidence department, I'll give him that."

After Ali jumped rope for fifteen minutes, Angelo had him move around the ring shadowboxing.

"Looking good. I'd like to see more head movement, though."

"Head's movin' fine. George can't touch this."

"I hope you're right because he's only got to catch you once."

"Stop whining and stop worrying. Whining and worrying."

Ten minutes later Ali was done.

"Heavy bag. Let's do six rounds, thirty-second break in between, combinations. Let's go. I want 'em crisp like your grandmother's piecrust. Let's go."

"Aww, why you gotta go mention piecrust? Now I'm thinking about apple pie." Ali laid a rapid one-two on the bag. "With ice cream," he said, sliding to his left, then ducking and throwing two left hooks into the body of the bag.

"Got me thinking 'bout blueberry pie," he said, giving the bag a jab-jab, cross ducking, and popping up with a left-right.

"Or maybe whipping cream," he added, throwing a quick double jab. "You got me all messed up, Dundee."

"Focus, please."

"I *am* focused. I'm Kodak focused," he replied, with a one-two. "I'm laser focused." He then hit the bag with a six-punch combination. "NASA ain't got no telescope that got the kind o' focus I got." He ended with a rapid flurry after the gym bell sounded. Two and a half hours later, they called it a day.

Muhammad once confessed that he largely took his public persona character from All Star Wrestling's Gorgeous George. He was outrageous, he boasted, he was flamboyant, and most fans hated him. When young Cassius Clay saw that, he was hooked. He knew how to play his image.

In "professional" wrestling, which contains a lot of acting, there is usually a baby face, a popular figure, and a heel who plays the bad guy. In Zaire, it was clear that Muhammad was the beloved baby face—they loved him in the African country. Angelo was awestruck by the reverence with which they treated Ali. He was like the Pied Piper the way they followed him everywhere.

Kids would chase the motorcade and chant "Ali, *bomaye*." Angelo asked one of their camp's handlers the meaning of the phrase and was told it loosely translated as "Ali, kill him." Although the words were harsh, Angelo appreciated the sentiment. It warmed his heart that the man who was once kicked out of boxing for his beliefs, which Dundee agreed with, was now celebrated. Ali truly was the people's champion and Angelo was proud to be a part of his team.

Both Foreman and Ali kept camps for several weeks in Zaire. Neither wanted to lose the fight because he wasn't acclimatized to the region. The trip had many ups and downs due to the promotion by Don King. Schedule changes were almost daily with the production team and rumors flew that King had financing difficulties. None of this surprised Angelo, and although he'd never say as much to the press, he always felt that Don King was slippery.

Aside from the rumors and fears that the fight would not come to fruition, Angelo settled into Kinshasa, Zaire. The training, hotel lodgings, and logistics were all fine until a call came in from Foreman's camp. Angelo was forced to call a meeting.

"Thank you all for coming," Angelo said, looking out at Ali's huge entourage. "As you all know the fight is scheduled for September 25th. But this is boxing."

The room filled with murmurs.

"I got a call from George's camp. Apparently, he's suffered a cut on the face." The room began to moan and groan. "He got caught by one of his sparring partners."

"That's 'cause he's so slow," Muhammad bellowed, causing the room to erupt in guffaws.

"Fellas, ladies, the cut is, ah, near the eye so—"

The room grew loud. Everyone knew this meant four to six weeks. A cut to a civilian's face and he'd be good to go in a couple days, but to a fighter—different story. If a fighter's cut hadn't properly healed, it could be opened at any time during a fight. If the bleeding didn't stop, it could cost the fighter the match. Foreman would be allowed time to heal, simple as that.

"Aw, man," Ali barked, "are you sure that big oak tree didn't cut himself on purpose, out of fear?"

Angelo knew it wasn't a serious question and kept on. "If any of you need to make arrangements with loved ones back home I suggest you start working the telephones."

The meeting began to break up.

"The upside is that the concert with James Brown, Celia Cruz, B. B. King, and others is going ahead as scheduled. But don't anybody go over-indulging just because we've got a new fight date!"

"Yes, Dad," one of the group members called, garnering a few laughs.

Angelo had to smile at that one. "Last thing: if anyone absolutely needs to be stateside before the new fight date, which will be as far as six weeks out, come and see me. Welcome to the fight game, everybody. This is nothing new. Thank you for your patience and dedication to this team. That's all for now."

People shuffled around and grumbled.

"Muhammad, please hang back a moment. We need to plan out your training week by week up to fight night."

The weeks during George's recovery went surprisingly fast. Angelo dug into the culture, loving the kindness of the people and enjoying the food. He even managed to pick up a handful of phrases. The locals often laughed when he attempted to speak their language but they seemed to appreciate the effort he made.

He particularly admired how excited the people were to have Ali on their soil. They truly felt blessed that Muhammad was there.

Two and a half weeks had gone by when Angelo got word that the fight would go ahead on October 30, 1974. In the final two weeks he dug everyone out of vacation mode and into the fight preparation. The extra time allowed them to study George's tapes.

He, Muhammad, and few others went back and forth between the Foreman-Frazier fight and the Foreman-Norton fight. At one particular spot during the Norton fight, Angelo stopped the tape. He looked over at Muhammad and noticed a look come over his face—he'd seen it too.

"You caught that, didn't you, Ali?"

"You bet your favorite plate o' pasta I did."

"What?" asked one of the other spectators.

"Tell him, Ali."

"Look at the angle George hit those guys with, other than his hooks."

The other men waited. Angelo took over the dialogue.

"George punches downhill 'cause those guys are short. I bet he gets twenty percent more power throwing those bombs like that. It's devastating."

Ali cut in. "But me and George are both six feet two inches, which means he'll be punching straight. Even if he does connect, it's not gonna affect me like those boys. Look at that, his overhand right started up in the attic and ended in the basement. Joe didn't have a chance."

"That's right," Angelo added. "You're gonna slip those punches."

"Slip them punches," Ali parroted, getting to his feet.

"You're gonna block those punches."

"Block them punches," Ali now sang, and shadowboxed.

"You're gonna use your speed," Angelo said, getting to his feet.

"Speed—bop, bop, bop,"

"Reflexes," Angelo almost shouted.

"Reflexes," Ali shouted, and boxed around the suite.

"And you're gonna knock him out in ten!" Angelo shouted.

"Gonna knock him out in eight!"

"Eight? Ten, Ali," Angelo corrected.

"It's gonna be *here* in *Zaire* and it's gonna be *great* when George fall in *eight*!" Ali asserted.

"I'll take that," Angelo laughed.

As the fight got closer, publicity and interviews ramped up, as did all demands on Ali. Angelo was worried that his fighter was over-extending himself.

"You need your rest, Ali," he would say, but it had no effect. Angelo could only hope that Ali knew the depths of his stamina because George Foreman would be his toughest opponent.

The fight was slated for four a.m. so that a live simulcast could be shown in the United States, and the time finally arrived. The stadium, which was called Stade du 20 Mai, was packed to capacity with 60,000 people. Cheering commenced for George; after all, he was the reigning champion. But the crowd absolutely roared when Muhammad Ali took to the ring. Angelo wished he'd brought earplugs. He almost felt sorry for George, as it was plain who was the heel and who was the baby face.

When cornerman Bundini Brown saw Foreman across the ring he uttered, "Damn, Ang, he looks like a killer."

"Oh? I think the ref looks quite tame," Angelo said, attempting to downplay the the feeling that he too shared. Bundini laughed nervously at the joke.

Ali came out at the opening bell, floating like a butterfly, as boasted. He flicked his jab at will, popping George in the face. Faking a jab, Ali threw a straight right hand, catching Foreman flush. The crowd roared approval. George, seven years Ali's junior and the favorite by two and a half times, became visibly frustrated.

"Uh-oh, he's poked the bear, boys," Angelo shouted to his cornermen.

George had no answers for Ali's speed. Still, he pressed forward, although not bobbing and moving like Joe Frazier. George moved like a slow-moving robot with thunder in both hands. Eventually, he cut the ring down on Ali, pinned him against the ropes, and went to town.

"Get off the ropes!" Angelo shouted, knowing his cornermen barely heard him, let alone his fighter. Ali mostly took the shots on his arms or leaned back on the ropes, causing Foreman to miss. This was good news, but still . . .

"Get out of there, Ali. Slide out!"

The bell sounded. Round one was in the books and Ali took it. Once in the corner, Ali said, "Can't keep that up all night, that boy's strong."

"Just stick to the plan and we'll take this belt, you'll see."

"Change of plan," Ali said, getting off the stool. The bell sounded.

"Change of—what change? Muhammad!"

The bell sounded. Ali leapt from the corner and continued peppering George with decent shots. Still, George moved forward and managed to put Ali on the ropes. George's big, arcing hammer-fists swooped down like catapulted boulders. Ali took some hits and blocked some hits. It was difficult for Angelo to watch.

"Off the ropes, Ali, come on!" he cried. To his cut man he shouted, "Geez, those ropes sure have a lot of give. Muhammad looks like he might tumble out of the damn ring!"

Ali made it through the next couple of rounds.

"I know you're an improviser, Ali, but I can't say I'm loving what I'm seeing."

"I got 'im. I got this guy."

"Stick and move, and I'll believe it."

It was the middle of the fourth round when the light bulb went on above Angelo's head. He allowed himself a smile. *He's going to let George punch himself out. That's why he's leaning on the ropes. Look at George, he's panting like a border collie!*

Rounds five, six, and seven went by in much the same fashion. George looked like a bear nearing the end of a marathon.

"Go take him out, Ali. He's ready to go," Angelo said confidently.

Ali met George head on. Jab, cross, double jab, straight right. George staggered, throwing lifeless punches that missed by a Louisville mile.

"He's all yours, take him out!" Angelo shouted, although his voice was nearly gone.

Ali put together a final combination with surgical execution. George Foreman went down. For a moment it appeared he might gather his feet beneath him, but only for a moment. He was done. By the middle of the eighth round, Muhammad Ali was once again the undisputed heavyweight champion of the world!

People descended on the ring. The 60,000-strong crowd lost their minds with excitement. It was as if all of Africa had won the title. Angelo's eyes filled with tears as he rushed to his friend and champion. He helped Bundini hold him up. Ali's arms were in the air.

"I am the greatest," Ali shouted. "Two-time champ. I am the greatest!"

Angelo got his ear for a second. "You did it, champ. You did it!"

Everyone was laughing and crying at once.

"*We* did it, Ang. *We* did it!"

Chapter Ten

JOE FRAZIER: AND SO WE MEET AGAIN

In the weeks following the fight, Ali's technique of leaning on the ropes and allowing George to punch himself out became famous as the "rope-a-dope." Angelo liked the poetry of the term although he thought it a bit harsh referring to George as a "dope." Still, if a man willingly agreed to do all of the heavy lifting, which later contributed to his demise, so be it. This was a competitive combat sport, after all.

Muhammad rocked Angelo one evening during a phone call. "I'm thinking of retiring."

Because a fighter's emotions can be all over the map after a loss, as well as a win, Angelo restrained a sigh and took a matter-of-fact approach.

"Champ, the run-up to a goal is huge. There are the hours of preparation, the roadwork, training, nagging injuries, press, and so much more. I don't need to tell you that. But something they never tell you fighters is that achieving a goal can leave an empty feeling where your drive once was."

Ali pushed back. "What's next? What else is there?"

"Come on. Sometimes it's easier to chase than to accomplish. Fighters are often hungrier during the hunt for the strap than when it's around the waist. Everybody and their dog are coming after the belt holder and they're hungry! That is why some managers overprotect their belt-carrying champ. It's not always about money. It's that they see their guy has lost that spark. Am I making sense?"

"I'm hearing a lot of psychobabble, but you makin' sense. I always said you talk too much."

"I'm not done, so button it. You need to take more time, and by that I don't mean ballooning up in weight either."

"I'm a svelte two hundred and fifteen pounds. And pretty, I might add. Gonna stay that way too."

"Careful. There's an adrenaline dump after a fight. Longer term depression can set in once a victory has been won and 60,000 screaming fans have gone home. It's human nature. Take some time, stay in shape, and keep fighting, because I believe you are the greatest. But if you really feel empty and can't shake it, then by all means retire. The ring is no place for a guy who isn't sure what he wants. That guy goes to sleep in a hot hurry."

"Some wise words, thank you. I'll sleep on it."

"That's all I ask."

"But if I don't retire and we keep working together, you gotta stop talkin' so much."

Angelo heard laughter before the line went dead.

"That kid never stops," the trainer said, shaking his head as he put the receiver on the cradle.

～

Muhammad decided to remain in the game and took on a handful of challengers. By May of 1975, nine months into the presidency of Gerald Ford, Ali was slated to fight Ron Lyle at the Convention Center in Las Vegas, Nevada. Lyle was a big man but possessed slower hands as well as inferior footwork to Ali. He'd also rung up only seven wins by knockout. He should not have been a problem. But Angelo noticed a change. Along with Ali's advancing age, his heart didn't appear to be 100 percent on board.

During what should have been a relatively easy fight, Ali found himself behind on points by the tenth round. He'd tried the rope-a-dope but obviously Lyle had seen tape of the infamous "Rumble in the Jungle"—he wouldn't bite when Ali tried to lead him to the ropes.

From the corner Angelo murmured, "We didn't fly all the way to Zaire just so you could come back and hand your belt to this guy. Now get it done, Ali. Dig deep."

Ali marched to the center of the ring and fed Lyle a barrage of punches. He maneuvered him into the neutral corner and went at him. Pausing, he called the referee over to stop the fight. The ref refused. Ali went back to work. The next time he called the referee over, the man called for a stoppage. Ron Lyle could take no more.

The victory was bittersweet, as Lyle's trainer was Chickie Ferrera, Angelo's former training mentor from back in his New York days. After the fight, the two trainers went for a drink and reminisced about the times past, as well as the future of boxing. It was a great night, and at its conclusion Angelo thanked Chickie profusely for his help and friendship.

Retirement was a subject that Ali brought up now and then.

It seemed to be on his mind until one day when a brainstorm hit him.

"Frazier!" Ali shouted.

"What about him?" Angelo asked.

"My next fight. Think about it. The world needs to know who the better fighter is. Well, they know it's really me, but they need to know for the record. We're tied right now. Let's break that. Set it up. Make it happen."

And there it was, another goal. Ali had found his prey and now he was going to stalk it. Thank God. The "Louisville Lip" fired up on all cylinders leading up to the third Joe Frazier fight.

"When we fight in Manila it's gon' be a thrilla. And I'm gon' whup that gorilla in the thrilla in Manila."

Angelo wasn't fond of having Frazier referred to as a gorilla, but he was a trainer, not a publicist. He did what had always worked—keeping his head down and working like Dad Merina taught. Sometimes that was easier said than done.

Muhammad had been seen around Manila with a woman who was not his wife. Rumors spread. Any time Angelo heard the camp whispering, he hushed them with a caution to get back to work. He had no desire to be a mother hen but he would not tolerate anything that threatened to derail the focus of the fight at hand.

When a reporter at a press conference asked about the "other woman," Ali danced around the question, but nobody was fooled.

After one training session it seemed Ali had decided it was time to do some explaining. He told his entourage to wait outside. Angelo remained with a patient and open expression on his face.

"What's up, champ?" he asked.

"What do you think about that reporter, the one who asked that question?"

"I think we're here to beat Joe Frazier a second time. I don't like non-boxing-related questions." Angelo turned to go. He wasn't comfortable having this conversation.

"What do you think? I mean, you been hearin' the rumors?"

Ali wanted to know if his trainer was affected by the news, now that the cat was out of the bag. He might have been seeking some sort of blessing as well.

"It's like this, champ. I love my wife unconditionally and I happen to respect the sanctity of marriage. Have I ever noticed other pretty women out there? Sure. But I'd never jeopardize what I have with Helen. As for you, I won't judge. Do what you want with your life. I leave that for the guy upstairs, *capisci?*"

Ali waited, as though he expected more.

"I understand your plight to a certain degree. Heck, you can't get five feet anywhere we've ever been without a dame sliding up to you. You're literally catnip to women."

"But you'd never—"

"Never in a million years."

The champ mulled the words over.

"Let's just stick to boxing, you and me," Angelo said, patting Ali on the back.

The next day Ali's wife arrived unannounced. She'd heard the rumors back home, and had hopped on a plane. Boxer and trainer were going over strategy when she showed up. After a brief hug hello, Angelo excused himself.

He hadn't cleared the hotel room when the row started. Shouts started coming through the door. Angelo couldn't remember the last time he moved so quickly as he hightailed it down the hall to his room. He popped the door open, jumped in, closed the door, and locked it. What happened outside the training ring had to stay there.

Fight night finally arrived. In Ali's mind, Frazier's career was nearing its end. Joe's body was tiring, his stamina was failing. Who better to retire him than Ali? For two rounds, the fight went in Ali's favor. He landed a series of combinations. But in the third round, Frazier muscled Ali into the ropes and caught him square in the jaw. Three people in the arena knew beyond a shadow of doubt that Ali was hurt: Frazier, Dundee, and Ali. The next four rounds went to Joe Frazier.

Between rounds Angelo chose his words carefully. "Champ, the rope-a-dope will not work this time. Joe is too accurate and his stamina is way stronger than we figured. Go outbox him."

Ali got up on the balls of his feet and brought the fight to Joe. He peppered Joe's face with jabs and crosses. But the intensity was impossible to sustain. Joe moved forward. From Angelo's perspective it seemed that Joe had been enraged so deeply by the pre-fight hype that he was a man possessed.

By the twelfth round, Ali dug into the reserves of his gas tank. He was fighting from the heart at this point. Picking up the pace, he tagged Joe. *Bam! Bam! Bam!* Joe's left eye closed. The right eye wasn't looking much better. Still, Frazier did not quit. He just kept coming for Ali, who kept up his precision combinations. Both men seemed held up by will alone. Round fourteen came to an end.

Ali flopped on the stool. Looking across the ring, Angelo hoped to read the opponent's corner language. A seasoned trainer can glean much from the other side's huddle, not unlike a military officer interprets Morse code. They seemed frantic. Something wasn't right.

"Hang on," Angelo said, putting a hand on Ali's shoulder.

Then the referee walked to Frazier's corner. There were hushed words, concerned looks. Eddie Futch, Joe's trainer, made the call: Joe Frazier was not coming out. He could not continue. It was all over.

Muhammad was declared the victor. As 60,000 fans screamed in delirious delight, Ali proved that, once again, he was right.

Chapter Eleven

FIGHT ON, MOVE ON

Ali decided to stay in the game. One day he and the Dundee family enjoyed lunch at Sal's, a favorite Italian restaurant. Sal, the owner, took every opportunity to trade banter with the table.

"Hey, Ang, how come it take-ah you so long before you bring-ah the champ in here?" Sal asked with a broad smile.

"What do you mean? The champ's bringing *us*. He's the guy with all the dough."

"You settin' me up, Dundee?" Ali said, pointing a fork. "I come out here for a nice lunch and you stickin' me with the check? You know about this, Helen?"

Terri and Jimmy, now young adults, laughed at Ali's shocked facial expression. They knew all about his playacting.

"No, no, Mr. Ali," Sal said. "I insist. Angie gonna pay and he's-ah gonna tip big too, right?"

"I've got a tip for ya—don't overcook the pasta," Angelo said.

Sal moved in and mock-strangled Angelo. After the laughs subsided, Muhammad signed an autograph for Sal.

When the high jinks settled down, Jimmy had a serious question. "Muhammad, what are your thoughts on Norton's crossed-arm defense?"

"Move laterally, come around, and work his ribs," Ali said in between chews.

"I like that," Jimmy said. "Because if you do that long enough, that crossed-arm defense will drop, leaving the head open."

Helen smiled. "I do believe that's right!"

Ali nodded at Helen. "I always knew you were the beauty in your marriage, but I didn't know you were the boxing genius too."

"You should pay closer attention," she chuckled.

"Listen to you two," Angelo said, shaking his head. "But yes, you are right, Jimmy. I like this plan. Remember, Norton is best when he moves forward."

"Uh-huh," Ali said. "With that step-drag thing he does. Them critics think I'm gettin' old but I got Norton's number."

"I have no doubt," Helen said.

Ali leaned back in his chair. "We need to talk about camp."

"What about it?"

"I'm moving it to Miami."

"We're in Miami, champ."

"Miami, Arizona."

"There's a Miami, Arizona? What's in Miami, Arizona?"

"Other than camp, I have no idea."

Angelo pushed back in his seat and said, "I bet there's not one decent Italian restaurant out there. What am I gonna do for pasta?"

"I gotta lottsa pasta here. You wanna more?" Sal called, homing in like a pigeon on the word.

"Maybe Sal delivers," Ali teased.

Angelo packed up and moved to Miami, Arizona, to get his guy ready. Ali wanted some distance from the fans and the news hounds. Camp was set up at the Show Low Airport. It was all hangars and runways, and provided next to zero distractions— Angelo appreciated that fact.

Although they worked hard, a handful of sportswriters allowed at camp noticed that Ali seemed to have lost a step. They didn't keep it to themselves; they wrote about it. Their consensus was that the Frazier fight had taken a serious toll on the heavy-weight champ. Skeptics believed Ali was becoming banged up.

Ali and Norton had won one fight each: Norton won the first fight in March 1973 and Ali won the second contest in September of the same year. Because they were one and one, they needed a "rubber match" to break the tie. The fight took place in Yankee Stadium on September 28, 1976, in front of 30,000 raucous fans. It was close, and moved in a seesaw battle.

But Ali's legs weren't what they once were. He seemed slightly sluggish. Furthermore, he was leaving his chin exposed. He never had been one to lay his chin out for the taking. Norton was relentless but Ali dug deep, moving each heavy step out of sheer guts and grit. Each fighter gave as good as he got.

In the middle rounds, Ali took a vicious shot to the body that nearly doubled him over. Norton chased him and got Ali against the ropes. Fortunately, he recovered and moved out of danger.

Ali sat down heavily on the stool after the eighth round.

"Ya gotta watch that overhand right. He's bringin' serious heat with it. Keep moving your feet. I like what I'm seeing with the one-two; keep it up."

At times, Ali was able to get back on the balls of his feet and put together nice combinations. He wasn't doing much damage, though. Going into the final round, some brutal honesty was needed.

"You need to go for it, champ. I've got you even on the scorecards. Don't leave it in the hands of the judges. Definitive win, champ. Definitive!"

Ali did as instructed. Then Angelo noticed something odd with Norton. He was backing off. He wasn't pressing Ali.

"What's going on?" Bundini, the cornerman, asked.

"I can't believe it. His corner thinks Norton's ahead so they told him to get on his bike and ride."

"You're kidding."

Angelo grinned, then cupped his hands around his mouth. "Go for it, Ali, go, go, go. Now's the time, don't let up!"

Bundini joined in. Two voices were better than one.

Ali turned on the gas, drained his tank, and by the end of the fight it was his hand that was raised. He'd beaten another man who'd beaten him before.

"Never a dull moment working with this guy, huh?" Angelo chortled as he hugged Bundini.

It was 1977 and Jimmy Carter was president. A gallon of gas cost sixty-five cents. Ali went on to defend his title against Alfredo Evangelista, but later ran into a Mack truck named Earnie Shavers. Known as the "Black Destroyer," Shavers was regarded in some circles as the hardest puncher ever. From the early rounds it was obvious this was a brutal fight. Shavers was tough, no bones about it. It was not an easy win for Ali. The fight went the distance.

On Angelo's way out of the building after the post-fight press conference, he was cornered by a reporter he didn't recognize. "Quick question, Mr. Dundee. I'm sure you would agree that fight was too close for comfort. Any thoughts?"

"It's like the old adage says, and I agree with it, by the way. Some victories are harder than defeats!"

Following the Shavers fight, Angelo became concerned for Ali. Rather than float like a butterfly as he had in years before, he'd become more flat-footed. That meant he absorbed more punishment. Ali had completely cleaned out his division and beaten all who had once bested him, and some people advised him to retire. Angelo took a wait-and-see posture. Only a fighter can decide to fight or not.

Eventually, he decided to fight a young kid named Leon Spinks. The year before, Leon had earned a title as 1976 Olympic light heavyweight gold medalist.

Ali seemed oblivious to his own limitations, so Angelo spoke up. "Look, I don't care who you fight because I believe you can take any guy that gets in the ring with you. But you're not respecting this kid."

"What do you mean I ain't respecting Spinks? He needs to respect me."

"I mean you're dragging out there. You're not pushing yourself, not getting in enough roadwork. You're older now. This kid just won the gold. Think back to how you felt when you won—invincible, right?"

"Pretty much. But, look, this kid don't have my experience. He ain't been in my kinda wars. I know what I'm doing."

"We differ on that, I'm afraid. As your trainer, I gotta be honest. You're draggin' and that kid is coming for ya."

Helen and the kids had already gone to bed. Angelo read the sports section and when nothing in it grabbed his fancy, he placed it on the ottoman and let his mind wander back over the run he'd had with Ali. Together they'd had ups and downs, shared tears, bled more than a little, and above all shared a million laughs. February 15, 1978, was coming up fast. Las Vegas, Nevada, was when and where Ali would defend his title against Leon Spinks, a kid with only six professional fights.

CBS carried the fight and later announced that seventy million viewers witnessed the bout. As Angelo expected, the young Spinks kid came out firing on all cylinders. He mobbed Ali, never letting up. Ali attempted the rope-a-dope but Spinks was too strong, and punished him every time he tried the move. More than likely, Ali was merely trying to rest and recover.

Not only was the young fighter fast, he was tough. Ali's jab carried no pop, and his footwork was absent and combinations non-existent. It pained Angelo to watch. When the fight was over he was actually relieved, even though his good friend had lost.

The post-fight press conference was low-key.

"Muhammad, what are your thoughts on tonight's fight?"

The fighter leaned toward the microphones. "My strategy was off," he said. "The rope-a-dope was a bad idea. As a result, I let Leon rob my house while I was out to lunch."

A chorus of voices spoke at once until one reporter's rose above the others. "Angelo, have you got anything for us?"

"I was young when Ali came to me, and now," the trainer sighed, "I feel old with him."

The first day back at camp, Ali made a short speech.

"I own that loss. No excuses. If I hear anybody talkin' to

press giving excuses, you might as well pack your bags and get out. At the same time, anybody thinkin' the champ is gonna retire can use that door right over there." To emphasize the statement he pointed to the exit.

"I'm gonna get back in shape and whup that boy Spinks worse than his daddy ever did. Now, let's get back to work."

A Spinks rematch was set for New Orleans. Angelo was ecstatic. He'd never seen Ali train so hard. When he had a goal, the fighter achieved it 100 percent of the time.

Where Ali used to do four thousand sit-ups before a fight, now he did eight thousand. He also bumped his usual daily six-mile run in combat boots up to eight miles. The flab around his waist disappeared. Angelo was proud.

The chance to avenge his loss against Spinks was set for September 15, 1978, in New Orleans. Despite losing the first contest, Ali was a two-and-a-half-to-one favorite over the young fighter. The ABC Network paid $5.3 million for the television rights. From the opening bell, Ali landed combinations like nobody's business. He was back on his toes with a jab that pop, pop, popped.

At one point, Ali threw a four-punch combination, tagging Spinks all over head and body, then sleekly slid to his right. A dazed Spinks swung wildly but Ali was no longer standing where he'd been.

"Where did he go, Leon? Where did he go?" Angelo shouted from his corner. The other guys in his corner stared in shock. He wasn't one to taunt another fighter, ever.

"Knock it off, boys, I'm having fun out here," he retorted. "Look at him—the greatest is back."

When the final bell tolled, Ali won by unanimous decision, thus winning the title for the third time in his career.

Chapter Twelve

DO NOT GO GENTLY . . .

Back at home, Angelo relaxed in his favorite light brown lounger—a chair over which he and Helen had gone around in circles. She didn't want it to enter their newer, bigger Miami home, but her husband felt he should be comfortable, no matter what home he lived in. Eventually, she gave in when Angelo pointed out that he and the chair were both getting better with age.

"That statement is nonsense, but you were kinda cute when you said it."

At that instant the phone rang. Angelo pushed himself out of the chair. "I'll get it," he said. It was Ali.

"I want to fight Larry Holmes," he said pointedly.

It was conjectured that Ali might retire after the Spinks fight. And why not? He was a three-time champion and his body was getting old. Larry Holmes was not only the new kid on the block getting all the hype, but he was also Ali's former sparring partner. The training required would be incredible. The Holmes match would also be a seriously dangerous fight.

Angelo had learned over time that gladiators in gloves could have careers with several last hurrahs, with many endings and nearly as many new beginnings. In short, guys retired only to come out of retirement all the time.

But Ali had a new health wrinkle. His thyroid was giving him trouble and he had to be on medication. One night, after watching the late news, Angelo felt it necessary to give Doc Ferdie Pacheco a call.

"What have you woken me up for this time, Dundee?"

"Like you were sleeping," Angelo said. "I'm concerned with the thyroid medication Ali's on. He seems sold on them and claims he feels like a million bucks. Now, he may feel like a million bucks and look like a million bucks, but he's fighting at about twenty grand."

"Is he weak or having dizzy spells?"

"No spells, but his punch has lost nearly all its pep. The pop-pop-pop has gone, gone, gone."

"I was afraid of this."

"Afraid of what, exactly?"

"The thyroid medication is one thing, but we're talking about a prize athlete here. If it were you or me we could ride it out poolside."

"I see your point," Angelo sighed.

"I've always been straight with you."

"I appreciate that."

"In all honesty, I think Ali should retire. It's not just his thyroid. I'm worried about his kidneys, and other things that may be going on with him. He's been in some wars like no one else!"

"I'm sure he'll come around to retirement soon, but he feels he's still got some fight left."

"Yet you're calling because he's losing power."

"Come on, Ferd, I'm calling because of those damn pills."

"I don't know what to tell you. But I've gotta say it again. Retirement, otherwise . . ."

"Otherwise what?"

"I'm not sure how much longer I can be part of this team. I feel Ali is in danger."

Angelo exhaled heavily. "I'll make sure he gets a full work-up from his primary."

"That would be good."

Angelo was about to say goodbye when the doctor hit him with another doozy.

"One last thing. I've shared my concerns with Muhammad. Just thought you should know."

"Including the retirement part?"

"We doctors are straight shooters."

"Thanks for this, Ferd. Talk soon."

The doctor's words weighed heavily on Angelo. He and Helen stayed up late discussing the situation. She agreed that Muhammad should have a battery of tests. Until then, Angelo set his mind to the task at hand.

When he spoke to Ali, he approached it with all the skill and experience he had to draw on.

"Ali, we're really going to have to use the science part of the sweet science. Tie Holmes up when you need to, no shame in that. When you see your opening, take it like it's your favorite meal."

Even though Ali passed the medical tests, the fight was a

disaster. He couldn't put anything together inside the ring and found no answers to the onslaught from Holmes. It crushed Dundee to see his fighter take such a pummeling from a younger opponent. After the ninth, referee Richard Greene asked both Ali and Dundee if they wanted to stop the fight. A proud Ali said no.

The next round was even worse. Holmes, being a class act, called for the ref to stop the fight. Finally, with eyes welling up, Angelo was the one to make the call. The fight was stopped. Limping to the corner with help, Ali looked at Angelo with puffy eyes. Through swollen lips he said, "Thank you." This was it, the end. The end of a long, triumphant era, and now was the time for Ali to announce his retirement. Only . . . he didn't.

After medical treatment and some rest, Ali was back on the phone.

"That wasn't me in there, Ang. It was those damn thyroid pills. I'm going to fight Trevor Berbick."

Angelo could only think back to the line his old friend Gene Kilroy had said, "You can beat everybody, but you can't beat Father Time."

Since the beginning of the sport, fighters have believed that they've got one more fight in them. Ali was no different. However, he was having difficulty securing a license to fight. The commission had concerns about Ali's age and the years of pounding he'd taken.

Finally, a license was secured and the fight was scheduled against Trevor Berbick for December 11, 1981, in Nassau, Bahamas. Angelo didn't feel good about the fight, and not just because of Ferdie's input. The fight had practically the worst promotion Angelo had ever been a part of.

The main promoter was a man by the name of James Cornelius—a character with a shady, criminal past. Somewhere during the lead-up to the fight, renowned promoter Don King demanded a piece of the action. The two men, along with a small security detail of the Cornelius team, had a meeting. Words led to fists and Don King was hospitalized. Cornelius denied the meeting ever took place.

Incidents like these left a bad taste in Angelo's mouth, especially because Cornelius was a member of the Nation of Islam—which put a spotlight on Ali.

Marone, Angelo thought.

The date finally arrived. Ali kept the fight close all the way to the seventh round, but not due to great boxing; rather, it was that Berbick was a far less skilled boxer. In the end, Ali slowed down and took a beating. Following the Berbick fight, reporters asked Angelo for comments.

"The less said about the Berbick fight, the better. Next question."

When everyone had cleared out, the thirty-nine-year-old Ali sat alone with his trainer.

"I couldn't show and now I know. Father Time got me."

Angelo put his arm around his friend. "I'm proud of you. Extremely proud, when I think back when you went from amateur to pro. Wow, look at what you've accomplished. You say you're the greatest and, honestly, I can't argue with that. I don't mind telling you that you're like a son to me, Muhammad."

Ali turned his head and looked at him with sadness. "Thanks, Angelo, for everything."

"Aw, now, look, you're making my glasses fog up," his trainer said, pulling them off and wiping his eyes. When he put them back on, he saw Ali's eyes had tears in them as well.

Chapter Thirteen

BOXING GETS A "RAY" OF LIGHT

After much reflection and a few false starts, Muhammad Ali left competitive boxing. His heart and legacy remained, never to be forgotten.

What was his trainer to do? For a while, a void was left in Angelo's life, despite the massive boost in his reputation as the guy who had trained "the greatest." Life rolled along. He had a loving wife, kids growing like weeds, and an impressive stable of fighters. It was a new day and a new generation.

Angelo was never one to make a habit of following amateur fighters but it was hard to miss the US Olympic boxing team in 1976—they took five gold medals. One medalist was Sugar Ray Leonard. Angelo had met him previously at a few fights. This young talent was well spoken, polite, and handsome, and he'd been told by none other than Ali himself that when it was time to turn pro, Angelo Dundee was the man, period.

When that day arrived, Sugar Ray signed Angelo as his manager and offered him 15 percent of the take. This was a risk on

Angelo's part as Ray was a nobody at the time, except for the gold medal, of course. In the beginning, Angelo received 15 percent of nothing.

As usual, Angelo started the young fighter with an evaluation. Ray entered the 5th Street Gym wearing a face full of business. They began with sparring. As Ray warmed up, Angelo took out a pen and jotted down notes on the back of an envelope. The notes were few. The kid was fluid, moved well, was light on his feet, and had a good jab. Sugar Ray had a lot of promise, but definitely needed a few tips.

"Moving from amateur to pro is no easy feat, my friend," Angelo said. "We're going to build the perfect beast. Number one is stamina, seeing as you're going from three-round fights to fifteen."

"Yes, Mr. Dundee."

"Ha. It starts with Mr. Dundee but it'll be Angelo or Ang in no time. Just make sure it's nothing worse than that."

"You got it, Angelo," Sugar Ray said through his headgear.

"Aside from focus, hard work, and all that, you've got to be patient. Above all, patient. I'm not referring to the ring specifically; I mean with these fights I set up. We've got some distance to go before a title fight, but we will get there, I promise."

Sugar Ray nodded with an eager look on his face. Angelo had navigated these waters of breaking in a new guy a thousand times: same waters, different fighters. The sport evolved, and nothing stayed the same as each fighter followed in the footsteps of his hero, adding his own pieces to the pugilistic puzzle.

Ray worked hard and eventually battled his way to a title shot for the welterweight championship, with Angelo stealthily choosing the matchups. For the title, Sugar Ray's opponent was Wilfred Benitez, a hard-hitter who didn't have Ray's speed but was extremely dangerous in a sport where anybody can get caught by heavy hands. Angelo was ecstatic as Ray followed the game plan of unleashing rapid flurries, then retreating and playing defense when necessary. Ray stayed ahead on points, but Benitez was very tough and was not backing down.

By the fifteenth and final round, Ray sent a left hook at Benitez and caught him "on the button." Benitez toppled to the mat but got up quickly and took his standing eight count like a man. The referee signaled the fight to continue, so Ray moved in and threw a barrage of strikes that Benitez could not answer. At that point, the referee was forced to stop the fight. Sugar Ray Leonard became the welterweight champion of the world. Angelo Dundee had himself another champion.

Chapter Fourteen

HANDS OF STONE

By the 1980s, boxing had grown significantly as a sport. Television and pay-per-view were the latest and greatest, allowing millions of people to watch fights. The stakes were higher than ever, and money had worked its way into boxing to a degree that Angelo, the little kid from Philly, never could have imagined. He enjoyed the salary bump but he also knew, as a veteran of the game, that more money meant more problems. He couldn't remember the first time he'd read this biblical passage, but he knew it well: *For the love of money is the root of all evil.*

Sugar Ray got a lawyer named Mike Trainer who created Ray Leonard, Inc. The deal marked the beginning of a lengthy living nightmare for Angelo. All the changes to the sport with added money on the table meant his usual method of keeping the head down and focusing on the job wasn't going to be enough to get him through.

Now that Ray was making more money, his business team began to see Angelo as a threat. Suddenly, his 15 percent was too big a piece of the pie in the eyes of Mike Trainer and company. The hotshot lawyer used no subtlety in voicing his distaste for Angelo's contract, regardless of who was within earshot.

"We're paying you way too much, Dundee. None of the other trainers make what you make."

"If you don't mind, Mike, we're training," Angelo said, turning back to the ring to observe Sugar Ray's sparring match.

Trainer hopped onto the canvas and crowded into the corner.

Angelo stayed focused. "Side to side, Ray. Don't stand still, that's it," Angelo called.

Mike Trainer moved closer. "You're pretty much stealing from Ray. You know that, right?"

"Not now, Mike," Angelo said, feeling his temperature rise.

"Tear it up, Dundee. Tear up the contract."

Angelo ignored the annoying lawyer, while Carlos Sanchez, a recent lightweight added to Angelo's stable, stopped working the heavy bag and strode toward the ring.

"Hey, Mr. Lawyer, why don't you lay off? Can't you see they're working out?"

"Mind your own business, son," Trainer said to the young fighter.

"It's all right, Carlos," Angelo said. "I don't want your workout interrupted as well. Go hit the bag, please."

Carlos glared at the lawyer before returning to the heavy bag. Mike Trainer put a hand on Angelo's shoulder and whispered in his ear. "Tear it up, Dundee, I don't want to make legal troubles for you."

That was the last straw. "Trainer, I'd advise you to take your hand off me."

The lawyer removed his hand. "So you're threatening me now?"

"And if you ever touch me again you'll seriously regret it."

There will always be bullies in this world.

Trainer stepped down from the ring and spoke from the floor.

"You're overpaid. You're just a trainer. Try and remember that," he said. As the legal eagle turned to leave, he bumped into Carlos, who stood immediately behind him. Trainer jumped, slightly startled.

Carlos sneered in his face. "He stood by Muhammad Ali's side for three championships. Try and remember *that*, you cheap suit."

"Get outta my way," Trainer said, fast-walking out of the gym.

Carlos looked up to Angelo. "Can we ban him from the gym, boss?"

"Unfortunately not."

That evening Helen made gnocchi. Angelo practically salivated when he walked through the door. Helen set the table and joined her husband. He said a quick grace and ate quickly.

"Uh-oh," Helen said. "Bad day, sweetie?"

Angelo topped off Helen's glass, then his own, with Ruffino red.

"I tell ya, honey, this Trainer character is driving me insane."

"I'm sorry. Can you do anything?"

"A guy just wants to go to work and get his fighter ready, plain and simple. But this lawyer has no respect for anything but money. I've never had this kind of trouble before with any fighter, manager, or lawyer."

"Have you tried talking to Sugar Ray about it?"

"He won't talk about it. Says he wants to focus on boxing, not business."

"Makes sense," Helen said. "It's avoidance, mind you, but it makes sense."

"I'm not sure how to play this one because it can't continue like this."

"Sounds worse than the modeling industry," Helen said, putting a gentle hand on his. "I bet you're missing the good old days, huh?"

"I'm not really a guy who lives in the past, but I certainly miss the days when all that mattered was the sport. There was respect across the board for the sweet science." He paused. "Aside from the corruption, of course."

They shared a wry chuckle.

"But now these lawyers and leaches only see the money. It's killing the sport, babe, believe me," Angelo sighed. "It sure makes a guy think of a certain biblical quote, if you know what I mean."

"Money makes people funny, honey?" Helen smiled.

"Interesting version," Angelo laughed.

"Money is the root of all evil," they said in unison.

"*Salute bella mia, ti amo*," Angelo said, raising his wine glass.

"*Salute, bello*. I love you too."

Sugar Ray's first title defense was against Dave "Boy" Green, originally from the United Kingdom. Ray took Green out in the fourth, but what happened after the fight was not in the boxing trainer handbook. As the cornermen and Sugar Ray were heading back to the dressing room, Angelo heard a loud noise from behind, then saw a brief flash of bright light. He awoke with his corner guys and Sugar Ray looking down at him.

"What's going on, guys? Why am I laid out here on the table?" Angelo asked.

The fight doctor leaned over him. "How many fingers?" he asked.

"What are you doing here, doc? Three fingers, by the way, but what—"

"You got sucker-punched from behind," Ray said, quietly.

"Sucker-punched? By some crazy fan or what?"

"It was Cub Jacobs," Sugar Ray said.

"Cub? Your old trainer? Why in the hell would he—?"

"Jealousy. He's jealous of you training me," Ray said sheepishly.

"Well, if that don't beat the band. Can I get up now?"

"Yeah, slowly, though. Take it easy," the doctor said. He shined a small pen light into Angelo's left eye, then the right. "You're good. Take a couple pain tablets if you get a headache."

Ray's next fight was with "Hands of Stone" Roberto Duran. Angelo did a thorough study of the tough street fighter with fifty knockouts. Many people picked Duran as the favorite due to his punching power, but Angelo saw something other scouts and critics missed: the majority of the men Duran took out were on the small side. He also believed that in terms of skill, Sugar Ray had the upper hand. His conclusion was that Ray could beat Duran if he fought the fight *his* way.

Since the days when Ali invented his particular brand of pre-fight hype, the talk had tended to escalate between fighters. But few had the style, poetry, and subtle humor of Ali. The taunting that followed Ali's heyday became more brutal and poorly thought-out. Unsurprisingly, Duran's pre-fight hype was crude and crass.

Angelo did his best to regulate Ray's temper. "Don't rise to the bait," he cautioned. Although Duran was outright rude, Angelo didn't foresee a problem until the day he got a call from a raging Sugar Ray.

"He's gone too far this time. I'm gonna kill him when I get inside that ring." Ray sounded frantic.

"Don't lose your cool, Ray. If you do, he's got ya beat because you'll make a mistake. It's a trap. Remember how angry Liston was when he fought Ali?"

"You don't know what he said to me about my wife, in *front* of my wife!"

"I can only imagine it was horrible. Look, I think the whole thing is outta hand and that there should be limits to what a guy can say to another guy. But, hey, I'm just a trainer."

"He threatened to do all kinds of, well, let's just say *things* to my wife. Then he made obscene gestures."

"I'm sorry, Ray," Angelo said, remaining quiet while the enraged fighter blew off steam on the other end of the phone with choice expletives.

Finally, Angelo gently interrupted. "I gotta go back to what I said earlier. If you go into that ring with this much anger, your game plan, *our* game plan is going to go out the window. You'll be handing that guy the victory."

On the other end of the line came a sound of frustration.

"Don't do it, Ray. Stay calm and beat him fair and square. Trust me, son, I've been here too many times to mention."

"Okay," Sugar Ray said, releasing a deep sigh. "I'll fight him fair and square, like you said."

"Good."

"But that sucka's gonna die in that ring, mark my words." Ray hung up the phone.

"That went well," Angelo said, putting the receiver in the cradle.

Helen gave him a look from across the room, where she had been staying quiet.

"I could hear it from here," she said. "Ray's coming apart, isn't he?"

"You could say that, sweetheart."

From the opening bell, Roberto Duran charged forward like a bull. In the corner, Angelo watched him barnstorm. It was a good strategy, because with Ray pushed against the ropes, his jab and footwork were neutralized. Speed was useless if a man couldn't get it off.

Angelo did what he could between rounds and Ray managed to battle back. But it was not enough. Duran completely mauled Ray, like a bear on an elk. Duran made Ray fight the fight that *Duran* wanted. Ray suffered the loss, but not without learning a lot.

"We live to fight another day," was all Angelo had to say after the fight.

Chapter Fifteen

I FIGHT NO MORE

After some rest and reflection after the Duran loss, it was time to resume training. Ray was waiting outside the door of the gym when Angelo drove up. They said quick hellos and went inside. As Ray geared up and stretched, Angelo had a few words to say.

"The best thing we can do at this point is learn from mistakes and understand everything Duran showed us."

Ray continued to warm up without interrupting his trainer.

"Duran treated you pretty cruelly on the lead-up to the fight. Once inside the ring, he put you on the defensive. None of that will happen in the rematch."

"Yes, sir," Ray said, staring straight ahead. He switched to skipping, still listening intently.

Angelo leaned against the side of the ring and folded his arms. "Do you know why Muhammad Ali was the greatest to partake in this game?" He didn't wait for an answer. "It's because when he got knocked down, he got up again. Specifically, when he lost, he always took the time to understand why. If he showed up out of shape and it cost him, he'd come back fitter and avenge the loss."

Ray gave a quick nod of his head and skipped faster.

"He never let a loss get him down and you can't either. We know Duran is going to taunt, so . . ." Angelo opened his arms wide, "let him taunt. Be the bigger man."

"He rushed in at me like a freight train," Ray said.

"So we move, we use our footwork, we use our intellect . . . which is what your idol was a master at."

"Yes, sir," Ray said, eyes forward.

"You're the better boxer. You're the smarter guy. So what are we gonna do on the rematch?"

"Win."

"I'm sorry, I didn't hear you," Angelo said, cupping a hand behind his ear.

"I'm gonna win with brains and skill!" Sugar Ray shouted.

"There's my guy. *Tutto bene amico*! That means very good, my friend."

"Yeah, I thought it was something like that," Ray smiled.

Ray would get the rematch with Duran, but first he had to fight Eddie Gant. As Angelo was wrapping Ray's hands in the dressing room, lawyer Mike Trainer entered. The team went silent. The lawyer walked up to Angelo.

"Sign this," he said, and thrust a yellow document in front of Angelo's face. Angelo couldn't believe the nerve of the pesky lawyer. Surely Ray would back him off. But Ray kept his head down and tested the wraps without uttering a word. The rest of the crew behaved similarly. The only sounds were throats clearing and shoes shuffling.

"Why do I get the feeling everyone knew about this little ambush but me?" Angelo said, looking around the room. No one met his eyes.

"Whatever, Dundee, sign it," Trainer said.

Angelo struggled to control his temper. "Do you realize we have a fight in less than thirty minutes? Back off and let me do my job."

"And this is my job. We're paying you too much. This is Ray's money. He's the guy in the ring, not you."

"Thanks for clearing that up for me."

"A hundred guys would take this job for free, Dundee, and do just as good a job as you."

"Said the boxing expert in the three-piece suit," Angelo retorted.

"Sign it."

Angelo checked the room a final time; no support, just silence. One thing he'd learned from his father was that a man's got to pick his fights wisely. And without the support of his fighter, Sugar Ray, what could he do? Sugar Ray was his boss—perhaps this was what he wanted.

Angelo snatched the paper out of Mike Trainer's hand and signed it.

"You win, Trainer. You've been hounding me for two straight years over a deal that was legally offered to me, *to me*! But it seems this is the way it's got to be played. Now, you have your document. Get out before I don't act so polite."

Angelo couldn't very well lecture his guys on the benefits of a cool temperament and then lose his cool. So he shook it off, fixed his mind on the fight, and helped Ray win the victory over Eddie Gant.

Up next was the rematch with Roberto Duran. Before the opening bell, Angelo looked across the ring and saw that Duran had lived up to his reputation as a partier and indulger. He obviously felt that he'd walk through Ray. In that moment, Angelo knew Ray was gonna take him. The bell rang and the two fighters met in the middle of the ring. This time, Ray fought his fight. He peppered Duran with jabs. Moving energetically, he put sweet combinations together. Duran became frustrated. The street fighter wanted to go toe to toe. *Sorry, pal,* Angelo thought, *you don't always get what you want.*

By the eighth round, Duran could be seen talking to the ref and walking around the ring, emotionally upset. Finally, both camps understood what Duran was saying.

"I fight no more," Duran said.

Duran quit! Sugar Ray Leonard avenged his loss to the scrapper.

After the fight, Angelo called Helen from a pay phone. He excitedly explained what had happened. "Ray was looking great and then Duran couldn't take it anymore. Some of the press got it wrong. Don't believe what you read in the papers, honey. They're saying Duran said, 'No mas,' when he said, 'I fight no more.' I actually feel sorry for the man."

"Why's that?"

"He was a good fighter but he did the unthinkable—he gave up a fight. It's career suicide. I mean, this one will go down in history. That's my prediction, anyway."

"That's one strange business you got yourself, Angie."

"Tell me about it. Love ya, doll."

"Love you too. See you soon."

Chapter Sixteen

THE HITMAN COMETH

Even though Angelo had signed Mike Trainer's document, the final details had not been fully hashed out. Trainer wanted to pay considerably less money than the prior deal, and even less than standard trainers made.

Angelo never understood the obsessive hatred the lawyer had for him. Still, he was raised to treat others with respect, no matter what. He'd raised his own kids under the same banner. But on more than one occasion, he wanted to punch the smug lawyer in his kidney.

Turn the other cheek, my backside!

The big matchup the boxing community wanted to see was Sugar Ray Leonard vs. Tommy "the Hitman" Hearns. But the commission wanted each fighter to undergo tune-up fights, which were to work as hype for the big matchup.

During his tune-up, Hearns walked through his opponent. Ray, on the other hand, had a tough nine-round brawl with Ayub Kalule before pulling off the victory.

Once again, Angelo put on his study cap for Hearns and learned that the long, lean fighter, with a wingspan just shy of an airplane, had mastered the art of dispatching his challengers. One potential hiccup was that Hearns's trainer, Emanuel Steward, had trained Sugar Ray during the amateur days.

How well would Steward remember Ray? Would he know what the opposing team had planned going in? These were the questions that Angelo pondered.

Rounds one and two were not easy. Hearns was difficult to get near. And when Ray managed to gain proximity, he had to get out in a hurry as the Hitman was incredibly dangerous. Almost every time Ray worked his way in, he'd receive a stiff jab for the effort.

By the middle rounds, Angelo was advising Ray to work Hearns's body. "Work the body and the hands will drop" was the old adage. It turned out to be true. Hearns lowered his hands and Ray came over the top with a hook. By the eighth, Ray had the upper hand. Over in the opponent's corner, Emanuel Steward was snapping his fingers in front of Hearns's face. He was dazed.

Just as the tides of the ocean shift, so do the currents in a boxing match. The Hitman came out firing and turned the tide in his favor. A seesaw battle ensued. By the twelfth, Hearns was in control and the same crowd that had been chanting for Sugar Ray was now chanting for his nemesis.

Angelo could feel the window of opportunity closing. Between rounds he came at Ray straight as an arrow—short and to the point. "You're blowing it, son."

That was all it took for Ray—he wasn't going to come this close and lose. He hopped off his stool and charged, pounding on Hearns for two more rounds. Ray knocked him down twice and then the referee stopped the fight.

The victory made Sugar Ray the unified welterweight champion. He defended that crown with an easy three-round bout, but later complained of blurry vision. After an initial visit to a doctor, Angelo went with Ray to the follow-up visit.

"Mr. Leonard," the doctor said, "I've consulted with two other specialists on your case because we take this type of issue very seriously."

"I appreciate that, Doctor," Ray said. Angelo could feel his fighter's nervousness.

"And it's our conclusion that you have a partially detached retina. We recommend surgery."

As the doctor broke down the procedure, Angelo sat back. If it were his child sitting in the office he would probably recommend he go along with the surgery and then hang up the gloves. He wasn't sure Sugar Ray would do that, though.

With the consultation nearly through, Angelo asked, "Doc, do you think he sustained this injury over time, or during his last fight?"

"In my opinion, it was that amazing fight with Tommy Hearns," the doctor replied. "Congratulations, by the way. Unfortunately, the win came with a price. Please let me know your decision."

Six months after surgery, Sugar Ray retired even though the doctors cleared him to fight again. This was his second retirement. The world had been calling for a fight between "Marvelous" Marvin Hagler and Sugar Ray, but once again, it was not going to happen.

Angelo turned to the rest of his fighting stable, worked hard, and enjoyed his family life. Two years into Ray's retirement he received a call from the former champion.

"It's me, Ray. I miss it. I love it. I'm coming back."

Angelo didn't have to think for very long. "Let's fire up the machine and do it!"

The first fight back, Ray found himself in trouble. He got knocked down in the middle rounds and was forced to take a standing eight count. He battled back and took the win in a later round.

Back in the dressing room, Ray lamented to his trainer, "I don't know . . . it's not there anymore."

Angelo knew better than to tell his guy "it's there" when only a fighter can know the truth about his confidence level. Ray retired . . . again. Angelo could not say he was surprised, because by this time he'd literally seen everything in the fight game.

In a short two years, Sugar Ray Leonard was back and ready to fight "Marvelous" Marvin Hagler.

Angelo dug deeply into research and discovered a "tell" in Hagler's footwork. The fighter would often take a step, or sometimes two short steps, prior to throwing a punch. Angelo revealed his findings to Sugar Ray.

"Really?" Ray asked with a slight smile.

"And that's not all, my friend. As you know, he fights as a southpaw," meaning as a left-hander.

"Yes."

"But he's not a *true* southpaw. He's actually right-handed, so we're going to change the direction of your movement."

Ray was incredulous, with eyebrows raised, but he said, "You haven't been wrong yet."

Angelo was not wrong, but he was very surprised to see a

turnaround: Hagler came out of his corner with a traditional right-hander's stance. Because of Ray's ability, he must have decided to move back to traditional.

Hagler kept the stance, even though Ray was "piecing him up."

With Ray back on the stool, Angelo tried to decipher why Hagler was continuing with what looked like a losing strategy.

"He must think he's ahead on points—too cocky. You've got this guy, Ray. Just keep fighting your fight."

He also recommended Ray finish the fight with a spectacular flurry of punches, which was a trademark Muhammad Ali flourish.

"Judges eat that stuff up," he added.

Ray did exactly that and ended with a lightning-fast barrage. The crowd went wild as Ray's hand was thrust into the air by the referee. At the press conference that followed, Hagler felt the judges had robbed him of victory. But the decision held and Sugar Ray Leonard proved that the unbeatable "Marvelous" Marvin Hagler could be beaten.

The warm glow of victory did not last long for Angelo when lawyer Mike Trainer reared his ugly head once again. He short-changed Angelo on the agreed payment for the fight.

That's the thanks I get? Angelo had never been treated this poorly in his career by any fight camp. He placed repeated calls to Trainer's office, receiving no reply. When he reached out to Sugar Ray, he still got nothing.

Further down the line, Mike Trainer finally called to demand that he attend a press conference.

"I'll attend your press conference when I have a signed contract from your side of the aisle, Trainer," Angelo responded heatedly.

"Fat chance," Trainer said before hanging up.

Angelo did not attend the press conference.

$\approx$

Sugar Ray Leonard went two out of five on his next fights, without Angelo Dundee in his corner.

The trainer and his wife were strolling the beach strand, enjoying the call of gulls and the smell of sea air, when she grabbed his hand. "If Sugar Ray had called you to corner for him in his last fights, would you have said yes?"

"If Ray asked, I would have done it, no question. I really love that kid." Angelo slid his arm around Helen's waist. "I'm sure his mind was poisoned by that thieving lawyer."

"You're a good man, Angelo Dundee, a good man. I wish you'd heard from him."

"Thanks, doll."

Chapter Seventeen

THE RETURN OF GEORGE FOREMAN

To Angelo, it seemed only yesterday that Terri had run around the living room, laughing while Jimmy played incessantly with his favorite fire truck. Now, the kids had grown into beautiful young adults. Still, he insisted that every Wednesday night be pizza night at Gino's when he wasn't working. The Dundees always sat at a round table near the back of the restaurant.

"When you were kids, you'd only eat cheese pizza," Angelo commented.

"Really?" Jimmy said. "I can't believe it."

"It's true, ask your mother."

"It's true," Helen replied. "Your poor father was beginning to think you weren't Italian."

"Scared me to death," said Angelo, chewing on a slice of meat lover's pizza.

Terri grinned. "But we grew up and expanded our palates, right, Daddy?"

"Good thing too," Angelo smiled. "It saved our marriage; I was beginning to wonder who your father was."

"Angelo Dundee, you stop right there. This is the dinner table," Helen laughed.

Jimmy topped his mother's Chianti and poured more for his father. "So, Dad, what do you think of George Foreman's boxing comeback?"

"I'm beginning to think it's more of a big deal than most people know. His last few fights were with some respectable guys. I hope he knows what he's doing because he's no spring chicken."

"Isn't he fighting your guy Adilson Rodrigues in a couple weeks?" Jimmy asked, setting down the Chianti.

"Would you like to corner with me on that one?" Angelo asked.

"It's kinda why I brought it up, Dad," Jimmy smiled.

"My sly big brother," Terri said, punching Jimmy in the shoulder.

Angelo chuckled. "It's going to be almost surreal standing across the ring from George after all these years. It'll probably remind me how old I am."

"You're still a young buck in my eyes," Helen said flirtatiously.

"Really?" Angelo grinned, sliding his chair closer to Helen's.

"Knock it off, you two," Jimmy said.

"Yeah, we may be grown, but we're still your kids," Terri laughed.

He'd taken the walk to the ring a thousand times beside at least a hundred fighters, but the sound of Angelo's own heart beating in his ears never got old. As the crowd swelled and growled, he was as nervous on that day as the first time he'd served as a bucket boy. He, Jimmy, and the crew climbed into the ring for the opening announcements. As they prepped the water, sponges, ointment, wraps, swabs, and more, George Foreman entered the ring.

Angelo froze and gently tapped Jimmy on the shoulder.

"Son? Jimmy? Son?"

"Yeah, Dad?"

"Look," Angelo said, indicating George Foreman.

"Holy mackerel, Dad, are you serious? He's huge."

"Massive. We're in trouble," he whispered, careful not to let his fighter overhear the dialogue. A quick shake of the head and he got back down to business.

Round one did not go well for Adilson. By the time he returned to the corner, Angelo saw fear in the man's eyes— he didn't blame him; he was fighting a giant, for heaven's sake.

By round two, it was all over. George laid Adilson Rodrigues out on the mat.

The mood was somber at the airport for Angelo and the crew. Rodrigues excused himself to grab a drink. What happened next was almost unbelievable: George Foreman slid down into the next seat.

"Hell of a fight tonight, George," Angelo ventured, slightly at a loss for words.

The big man had a smile on his face, just like the ones he'd worn in pre-fight press conferences. Angelo could not believe the transition. The last time he'd seen George in Zaire he didn't think that glowering mug was capable of forming a smile.

"I've been following you, Angelo—for years, in fact."

"I sure hope you don't have a beef," Angelo laughed nervously.

"Beef? Not at all. I've been watching your career and like what I see. Not just the wins, but I like the way you treat your fighters. You've got a dynamite reputation. I mean, look at your achievement with the great Muhammad Ali."

"Wait a minute, did you just refer to Ali as great? Are my ears hearing correctly?"

George let out a big belly laugh. "Life is a beautiful thing, isn't it? Praise God." He patted Angelo's leg. Looking down, two-thirds of Angelo's thigh had disappeared beneath Foreman's giant paw. "I want you to be my trainer. What do you say?"

Angelo studied his face and saw the big man was telling the truth.

"I was skeptical when you initially came back, but holy cow, I'm a believer now. I'd be happy to work with you."

George extended a hand.

"Just don't break it," Angelo teased, grasping George's hand.

Working with George Foreman was like rediscovering a love of boxing. The guy was a giant teddy bear of positivity—always. Being in the game as long as Angelo had, he rarely attempted to change what a fighter brought to the table, especially with a veteran of the game like George. Was he going to teach George how to rotate his fist and squeeze at the end of a punch? Heck, no. Foreman had cement blocks inside his gloves and he knew how to use them.

"Can I show you something, Angelo?" George asked with his larger-than-life smile.

"Sure."

"It's outside. Come on," George said, leading the way. He wore a gray hooded sweatshirt with the sleeves cut off, revealing arms that looked like Buicks attached to his shoulders. His loose black sweatpants were cut above the knee, allowing movement for his tree-trunk thighs.

Outside sat an old blue Ford F250 pickup truck with a crane apparatus bolted to the truck bed. Suspended from a sturdy hook was thick chain from which dangled an eighty-pound heavy bag.

"What do you think?" George smiled, extending an upturned palm like a game-show host.

"I think I've seen everything. What's the play here?"

"Andy drives the truck while I jog behind and put in the work."

A man nearly as big as George, and wearing a trucker's hat, said hello from the cab. He introduced himself as Andy.

"This is how I do it," George said. "Hop in. I think you'll find Andy's a real interesting guy."

"When in Rome," Angelo answered.

"If you have anything to say, like you want to tell me a strategy or you want me to raise my hook up, just ask Andy to pull over. You can hop right in the back and give me instructions from there."

"Sounds like a plan," Angelo said, jumping up into the truck and putting on the lap seat belt.

"Welcome aboard," Andy Simms said, starting the engine. "Quite the unorthodox setup, huh?"

"True. But George has knocked out twenty-three of his last twenty-four opponents. If this is how he does it, who am I to fix what ain't broke?"

The cab of the truck suddenly rocked forward. Angelo threw out his hand to brace against the dashboard.

"What the hell was that?"

"That's the next heavyweight champion of the world," Andy

laughed. "George just gave the bag a body shot. It means he's ready to go."

Angelo crossed himself and kissed the crucifix around his neck. Andy shook gently with laughter and put the truck in gear. They rolled along at about five miles an hour to start. Angelo peered out the back window. He couldn't see all of George, just the occasional massive arm coming around the bag, delivering body blows.

"Andy, my friend, I have now officially seen everything there is to see in boxing."

"Welcome to Big George's team, Angelo Dundee. Be prepared to smile, laugh, and gain a few pounds. Correction: a lot of pounds."

The interior of the cab shook again. It was almost as if George had heard the dialogue and approved with a hard right hand to the bag.

"You know why he's going to be champ? Because he fights for God. How many guys do you know do that?"

"There's a lot of religious guys in the game, Andy. I've trained more than a few."

"Yes, but George fights for God. I won't go into detail because I believe every man should tell his own story." He turned and held Angelo's gaze. "But if you get a chance, sit down with the man. You'll come away inspired, at the very least. Trust me."

"I'll be sure to do that. I'm already inspired by George. I thought his heyday was back in Zaire."

"Zaire! Now, that is a conversation I've been waiting to have with you since, oh, I don't know, 1974."

Angelo felt odd talking to a good friend of George's about a fight lost to the fighter he'd trained, but Andy made him feel at ease.

"No need to feel strange talking about this. George does all the time because it marked a turning point in his life. But again, you need to sit down with the man."

They'd been at it twenty minutes when Angelo asked Andy to pull over. "I want to try this riding in the back business."

"You're the trainer," Andy smiled, and tooted the horn two times.

Angelo got out and walked to the back of the truck. George stood with his hands on his hips. His massive chest heaved with exertion. Reaching into the truck bed, he grasped a one-gallon water jug and took a small sip.

"How ya holdin' up, George?"

"It's a beautiful day for training."

"You're looking good," Angelo said. "I'm gonna climb in back and check you out from here."

"Be my guest. I apologize that it's not too comfortable up there; we used to have a lawn chair but it never stayed put."

"I guess not with those bombs you're throwing."

"Sometimes when I hit this bag, I imagine I'm tenderizin' the steak I'm gonna eat later. Excuse me, steaks, plural."

"Whatever works for ya," Angelo grinned, climbing onto the wheel hub.

George called up to Andy. "Let's take it up a few mph's. I'm warmed up now." Then George hit the bag dead center one time. Angelo felt the blow and grabbed on to the side of the truck. George laughed. Obviously, it was a trick George had done before.

The run lasted ninety minutes in total as Angelo observed George's training style. Back at the gym, the two men sat ringside and chatted while the fighter's hand wraps were removed.

"After Zaire, I went into a real depression," George explained.

"I was a young cat and the baddest boxer on the planet. How many young fighters you hear that from?"

"Too many to count."

"Right, but losing that fight was the best thing that ever happened to me. It led me to the church and it was *there* that the anger was taken from my heart."

"So there was all-around anger? I thought you just hated Muhammad."

"I hated everything and everyone. A young man needs guidance, role models, and love, essentially. The church taught me to love myself and then I was able to love my fellow man."

"That's a beautiful story, George. I appreciate you sharing it."

"There's more if you got a minute."

"Of course," said Angelo.

"The church took me in, saved me. I wanted to give back but I had no money, so God turned on a light bulb above my head. He gave me the talent to put guys on the canvas."

"He certainly did," Angelo said.

"So I took some low-level fights making twenty dollars here, thirty dollars there, and I gave it all to the church."

"That's incredibly generous. I know the fighting circuit you're talking about. You must have seen some ungodly stuff down there."

"Let's just say it wasn't pretty. Suddenly, twenty and thirty dollars became fifty and sixty, and so on. But I wanted more, for the church. So I kept on using my gift and next thing you know, I'm beating better and better guys."

Angelo stood up and stretched his back and did a couple of neck rolls. He wanted to be comfortable for the rest of the story.

"Sore back? Here, let me help you," George said, getting up.

"It's nothing, just old age. I'll be all right."

"I've got just the thing. Turn around and hold your arms close to your chest."

"Really, George, I'm okay."

"It's not wise to refuse a man my size," George laughed.

"Oh, all right, just don't break anything, or you'll have my wife to answer to."

George got behind Angelo and wrapped his big arms around him at shoulder height. The next moment Angelo's feet left the ground. He heard two cracks from his back, then George set him down gently.

"Wow," Angelo said, working his shoulders around. "That was great. I feel like a million bucks. Thanks, George."

"My pleasure," George said, sitting back down.

"Tell me about this training method of yours. Who came up with it?"

"I did. My thinking is this. I'm an older guy," he said, counting off items on his big fingers, "I'm a big man, and I pack a mean punch."

Angelo nodded.

"I'm not going to dance around like Ali, I'm not going out there with a lightning-fast jab, none of that. What I need is stamina to get me into the later rounds. And I'm now a fighter who moves forward until I get you where I want you, then I put you to sleep."

"Meaning you're not going to let a guy come to you and counterpunch."

"Nope. George Foreman moves forward, baby, slow and steady. Most of the time I only need to lay my paw on you once."

A big smile spread across Angelo's face. "I can work with this."

"I'm glad to hear it."

Both men got up and headed toward the doors. Before

getting into his car, Angelo called over. "It's a great thing what you're doing for the church. Very commendable."

"God gives to me, I give to God."

"No truer words," Angelo said. "Thanks for fixing my back. See ya tomorrow, pal."

Working with George buoyed his faith in the adage "the Lord works in mysterious ways." Angelo cherished his days with George Foreman. Where Ali won over the press in his day by using poetry, George used self-deprecating humor, often focusing on his love of burgers and his all-round food obsession. Because of this impertinent style and that fact that he was getting on in age, George had many detractors. Still, he got his title shot against Evander Holyfield.

Evander, being the younger fighter, obviously moved better than George and was able to evade many punches by sheer agility. In the third, George took a nasty shot to the head that wobbled him.

"Hang on, make it out of the round, that's it!" Angelo called.

George's massive frame moved, swaying up and down as he sat on the stool, but Angelo knew his stamina would hold due to putting in many miles of running on blacktop and roadway.

"How bad were you rocked, George?"

"I'm good, thank you."

Geez, such politeness even in the heat of battle! "You're looking good, pal. Just keep doing what you're doing and unleash that big right hand. Lay him out!"

"Yes, sir."

The next few rounds were pretty much a "stand in the middle of the ring toe-to-toe slugfest." Evander threw everything he had at his opponent, but Foreman was a mountain fighting for the Lord. He took the blows and answered with as many devastating right hands. At one point George rocked Evander, nearly knocking him out. But when the decision came, Evander managed to edge George out. Regardless, Angelo felt that George was the big winner, and had achieved a huge accomplishment.

Back in the dressing room, George was mellow but still managed to crack the occasional smile. Angelo kept his comments light.

"George, I'm proud o' ya. You gave as good as you got. Evander is an extremely talented fighter. Don't hang your head, son. Be proud."

"Tonight was not my night, but it will be soon. I have no doubt about that."

"Damn straight!"

"After the post-fight press conference, we're going for burgers," George said. "If you and Jimmy and the family want to come along, you're more than welcome."

"Sounds like a great idea," Angelo said.

Angelo went back to two hours of roadwork with George, dividing his time between the front seat of the truck with Andy and the back of the truck with George. They were getting ready for Tommy Morrison, born in 1969, and therefore considerably younger than George. At one point, George was working the slow bag and signaled to stop the truck.

"Hold," George cried out. Andy braked to a stop. George put his hands on his hips and slowly paced in a big circle.

"Everything all right, George?" Angelo asked. Andy got out of the truck and joined the two men.

"I'm forty-four years old, boys. This Morrison fight will

be my last one. I'm going to knock him out and put that belt around my waist." He paused. "I just hope the belt fits. Let's go, Andy."

Andy got back in the truck and waited for George's signature right hand down the pipe. The truck shook. Angelo knew the time was coming when George would hang up the gloves, as part of him felt the sport was too dangerous for a man his age. Still, sadness crept into his heart. It always did when the end was near for a fighter he loved.

Just before the fight night, George publicly announced that this would probably be his last, which Angelo felt got the crowd even more in George's corner. The bout was titled "The Star-Spangled Battle."

Tommy Morrison was a hard hitter, but George was up to the challenge. The strategy was simple: fight George's fight. Tommy changed his usual come-at-you style, which forced George into being the aggressor. The fans began to boo Morrison, who continued to jab and run.

"Dang it, that Morrison is wracking up points," Angelo shouted at his corner.

George did his best to cut the ring off, but the quick twenty-four-year-old was elusive. George suffered a tough loss.

Angelo called Helen after the fight. He needed to hear her voice.

"I'm sorry that fight was the pits," Helen commiserated. "Morrison ran away all night. The ref should have made him fight."

"Technically, he was fighting. He was in and out, and apparently scored enough points. It's a real shame because George is sticking to his retirement."

"It's probably better for his safety, right?"

"Sure, but I know he can grab that belt. I feel it in my bones. I realize this sport is not based on feelings, but George is special. He can do it. Look at his story, for Pete's sake."

"I know, sweetie. Hurry home."

"You bet."

It was business as usual for Angelo the next several months. George kept in touch and even had dinner with the Dundees a few times. Hollywood called with a sitcom deal and George embarked on the life of a TV actor. Angelo loved teasing George about the career change.

"Ha, from biggest puncher in the game to a guy that sits in a makeup chair before playing make-believe."

"Keep it up, and I'll write a part for you."

"Go ahead, they'll probably throw me off the set. I've got a face for radio, not television."

A year passed, and George called Angelo again.

"I'm coming back. I didn't like going out on a loss."

"That's great. Have you been chasing that bag at all, or have you been getting fat on craft services?'

"You're talking to a svelte two-hundred-fifty-pound, burger-eating machine."

"Whoa, that's great. I bet you can't remember the last time you were that light."

"Nope, not really."

"Then let's get after it!"

Through good luck, the alignment of the stars, or the will of God, George secured a title shot with sitting champion Michael Moorer.

The fight was called "One for the Ages" and it was held in Paradise, Nevada.

Angelo entered the dressing room with his son Jimmy

trailing behind him, then stopped and stared at the way George was dressed.

"Whoa! I haven't seen those shorts since—"

"Zaire," George answered. "That's right, I haven't worn these since I fought Muhammad all those moons ago." He looked thoughtful. "When I was champ. And I'll be walking out of this stadium as the champ again, so why not wear these?"

"I like it. Very cool," Jimmy said.

"Thanks. You know, I nearly burned these after that fight. I went into a very deep depression. I was in a very dark place."

"And the Lord showed you the light. Isn't that right?" Angelo said.

George pointed at Angelo and winked. "Exactly."

"I agree with my son. Very cool, George."

The fight was a straight-up brawl. Neither fighter gave an inch, neither fighter backed off or backed down. The rounds were grueling and Angelo knew George was behind on the cards. By the eighth round, he considered asking George to turn up the heat but decided against it. George was a patient fighter, so why shouldn't Angelo be a patient trainer? He decided to hold off, but if nothing changed by the tenth round, he'd tell George to hit the gas.

In the middle of the tenth, George was still behind. Angelo began putting his words together for the between-round speech when George picked up the pace. He began scoring points.

"That's it, George, launch your—"

Angelo never got the words out. George fired a short right, catching Moorer flush on the chin. The referee ran to where Moorer lay sprawled on the canvas and began the count. George moved to the neutral corner. The ref continued counting. Michael Moorer struggled to get up. His eyes were unfocused.

"Eight, nine, *ten!*" the ref shouted, and waved his hands. It was all over. "Big George" Foreman, the burger-loving man of God, fell to his knees and buried his face in his big gloves. He'd done it. Angelo and Jimmy ran to him, each putting an arm around their hero.

George's body rocked with heavy sobs. Angelo's glasses fogged up. He laughed and cried in the same moment when he saw his son crying—he hugged both men harder. At forty-five years old, George Foreman became the oldest heavyweight to ever hold the belt.

Chapter Eighteen

THE ROAD WELL-TRAVELED

Sunday night. Plates were overflowing. Angelo's mind flashed to his mother's Sunday night feast. He marveled back at his young self, the little boy, and wondered why he was late so many times.

Dumb kid.

He gazed at Helen, his beautiful wife, and wondered again how he got so lucky. He wondered even more why she stuck with him so long. Helen was laughing at a story Jimmy was sharing. *She's so beautiful when she laughs.*

He wasn't really listening to the story. Instead, he was taking a moment to count his blessings. Jimmy and Terri had grown into wonderful, accomplished, and thoughtful adults. He floated back to his youth, a time when he didn't have two nickels to rub together, but he was happy. He had learned to dance, mastered the rudiments of the fight game, and even fought for his country.

His mind jumped to brother Chris, fifteen years his senior. Chris had barely known him, but still gave him a shot at life in the Big Apple, and later in Miami. What a ride! If not for Chris, he would never have met Helen, the kids wouldn't exist.

His mind drifted to his parents, two of the strongest people he'd ever known. Without their strength, love, and religious-based morality, he would have been eaten alive in the business of blood. He still missed them and accepted that he always would.

Angelo let his mind return to the present. He rejoined the group and waited for Jimmy to finish his story. After the laughter subsided, he raised his wine glass.

"A toast."

Glasses rose.

"I've had a wonderful career. I want to thank you all, especially you, Helen, for standing by me. I couldn't have done this without all of your love and support. I've traveled the world, trained hundreds of fighters, and won several boxing trainer awards. But the best part of all was coming back here. Back home to *mi famiglia*!

"*Amo la mia famiglia ora e per sempre, salute!*" he said. I love my family now and forever, cheers.

Angelo Dundee died in Tampa, Florida, on February 1, 2012, surrounded by his family. His wife of fifty-nine years, Helen Bolton Dundee, had died in 2010. Angelo will forever be remembered as a man of integrity who trained some of the greatest boxers of all time.

Angelo's Fighters

A COMPENDIUM OF PUGILISTS

For more than sixty years, Angelo Dundee trained some of the best professional boxers of his time, and was known for being a brilliant strategist and inspired cornerman. The formal name for a fighter is pugilist. The word pugilism means the art or practice of fighting with the fists, or boxing. Here are a few of the renowned pugilists who worked with Angelo Dundee during their careers.

Muhammad Ali (Cassius Clay)

Muhammad Ali was born Cassius Clay on January 17, 1942. His boxing life began at age twelve. Six years later, he went to Rome with the US Olympic team and won a gold medal in the light-heavyweight category. In February 1964, Clay silenced odds makers by beating the unbeatable Sonny Liston. He won the WBA, WBC, and lineal heavyweight titles.

In 1967, Clay refused to join the draft, citing religious

reasons. He was exiled from boxing and forced into a four-year appeal with the US government.

Coming up as a young fighter in Kentucky, he was known as "the Louisville Lip," based on his braggadocio style. Two notable fights include "The Thrilla in Manilla" (vs. Joe Frazier) and "Rumble in the Jungle," in Zaire (vs. George Foreman). Not only was Muhammad considered by most to be the greatest fighter to step into the ring, he was the most recognized sports figure worldwide. In 1984 he was diagnosed with Parkinson's disease.

During his career, and after hanging up the gloves, he became a respected activist and revered social justice warrior. His causes took him to Mecca twice, several African countries, Bangladesh, and Southern Lebanon. He boycotted the 1984 Moscow Olympics because of the invasion of Afghanistan, and in 1990 he traveled to Iraq and negotiated the release of American hostages. In spite of the results, he was criticized by then-president George H. W. Bush.

Angelo Dundee has been quoted as saying that Muhammad Ali was like a son to him. Ali passed away on June 3, 2016; several thousand people attended his funeral in Louisville, Kentucky. He was known for his quick wit and humor. While James Brown always said, "I'm black and I'm proud," Ali liked to tease, "I'm black and I'm pretty."

Carmen Basilio

Carmen was born April 2, 1927, and died November 7, 2012. He topped out at five feet, six inches tall, fighting as both a welterweight and middleweight. With Angelo in his corner, he defeated Tony De Marco in 1955 to capture the welterweight title.

One of his most notable fights was in September 1957, against legendary boxer Sugar Ray Robinson. Ray was thirty-six years old at the time, and some argue he was the greatest to ever lace up the gloves. The Basilio vs. Robinson slugfest went the distance and won the middleweight belt for Basilio. While in retirement, he worked for a time in a brewery before teaching physical education at Le Moyne College in Syracuse, New York.

Jimmy Ellis

Born February 24, 1940, Jimmy Ellis fought from 1961 to '75. He and Muhammad Ali were friends and sparring partners for a time. The single fight during which Angelo was not in Ali's corner was when he cornered for Ellis against "the Greatest."

When Ali was forced to vacate his belt, Ellis won an eight-man tournament for the WBA heavyweight title, beating Jerry Quarry in the final bout. In a unification bout of WBA and New York State Athletic Commission belts, Ellis went up against the powerful Joe Frazier. Frazier proved too strong, forcing Angelo Dundee to throw in the towel in the fifth.

Ellis retired at age thirty-five in 1975, leaving the sport with a record of forty wins, twelve losses, one draw, and twenty-four KOs.

George Foreman

It was January 10, 1949, when "Big George" Foreman arrived on the planet. He totaled seventy-six career wins; sixty-eight of them were by knockout. The 1968 Olympic Games in Mexico was the setting in which George received his gold medal. In 1972, "Smokin' Joe" Frazier was undefeated until he met George at "The Sunshine Showdown" in Jamaica. In 1976, Foreman's fight against Ron Lyle was called the fight of the year; fans who witnessed it saw five knockdowns in the fight.

Foreman left the sport for more than ten years before returning at age thirty-eight after experiencing a religious rebirth. Angelo Dundee expressed that there was something poetic in working with George; many years before he had been in his opponent's corner in Zaire.

At age forty-five, Foreman beat Michael Moorer and became the oldest heavyweight titlist in history. Today, George is an ordained minister, inventor, and spokesperson for a variety of commercial products.

Wilfredo Gómez

Wilfredo "Bazooka" Gómez was a tough Puerto Rican lightweight born October 29, 1956. He trained with Angelo Dundee for a time and at one point had accumulated an impressive thirty-two knockouts in a row. That earned him the number-three ranking for the knockout-record streak.

In retirement, Gómez moved to Panama and developed a drug habit, which he later kicked. He became good friends with Roberto Duran and helped train Hector Camacho's son, Hector Camacho Jr. Gómez earned a record of forty-four wins, three losses, and one draw.

Sugar Ray Leonard

Ray Charles Leonard was born May 17, 1956. He was part of the Fab Four, which included Roberto "Hands of Stone" Duran, "Marvelous" Marvin Hagler, and Thomas "the Hitman" Hearns.

The four were lethal fighters who fought each other throughout the 1980s. Leonard won a gold medal at the 1976 Montreal Olympics and later was named Boxer of the Decade in the 1980s.

Leonard adopted the name Sugar after boxing great Sugar Ray Robinson. His fight style was similar to his idol, Muhammad Ali. Working shoulder-to-shoulder with Angelo Dundee, his first world title was captured in 1979 against Wilfred Benitez. After many retirements and returns, his impressive career had thirty-six wins, three losses, and a single draw.

Willie Pastrano

Willie Pastrano was born November 27, 1935, and began boxing at age sixteen. He and Cassius Clay were stablemates under Angelo Dundee, and often teased each other about who would be crowned champion first. Pastrano had a smooth style and strong left hand. He loved boxing but he had a slight aversion to training, and loved partying and carousing.

In retirement, he became the official host of the Presidential Steak House in Miami. He also enjoyed a short film career from 1967 to '71 and appeared on *The Jackie Gleason Show*. He passed away on December 6, 1997.

Luiz Manuel Rodríguez

Luiz Manuel Rodríguez was born in Cuba on June 17, 1937. He could fight in the traditional style or as a southpaw. He worked with Angelo first in Cuba as part of the "Cuban Connection," then later in Miami at the 5th Street Gym. Rodríguez liked to fight in the middle of the ring. He won both welterweight championships—in Cuba, as well as in the US Undefeated for thirty-six fights, he finally lost a split decision to Emile Griffith. Rodríguez was part of Angelo's fight stable during the same time Willie Pastrano was with the trainer.

About the Author

Jonathan's book *The Big Crescendo: A Lou Crasher Mystery* will be released in 2019 with Down and Out Books. His second book in the Crasher series comes out in 2020, also with Down and Out Books. He has two short stories in the *Palos Verdes Library District Anthology 2016* and *Palos Verdes Library District Anthology 2017*, and his story "Three Fingers of Scotch" is published in *Out Of The Gutter* online magazine.

Brown has taken a short story and expanded it to novella length. The story is based on his character Doug "Moose" McCrae, an ex–football playing nightclub bouncer turned amateur PI. Brown hopes to indie publish the book by Christmas 2018.

When not writing, personal training, and teaching drums, Brown enjoys life in sunny Los Angeles with his lovely wife, Sonia.

NOW AVAILABLE FROM THE MENTORIS PROJECT

America's Forgotten Founding Father
A Novel Based on the Life of Filippo Mazzei
by Rosanne Welch, PhD

A. P. Giannini—The People's Banker
by Francesca Valente

The Architect Who Changed Our World
A Novel Based on the Life of Andrea Palladio
by Pamela Winfrey

Breaking Barriers
A Novel Based on the Life of Laura Bassi
by Jule Selbo

Building Heaven's Ceiling
A Novel Based on the Life of Filippo Brunelleschi
by Joe Cline

Building Wealth
From Shoeshine Boy to Real Estate Magnate
by Robert Barbera

Building Wealth 101
How to Make Your Money Work for You
by Robert Barbera

FUTURE TITLES FROM THE MENTORIS PROJECT

A Biography about Rita Levi-Montalcini
and
Novels Based on the Lives of:
Amerigo Vespucci
Andrea Doria
Antonin Scalia
Antonio Meucci
Buzzie Bavasi
Cesare Beccaria
Father Eusebio Francisco Kino
Federico Fellini
Frank Capra
Guido d'Arezzo
Harry Warren
Leonardo Fibonacci
Maria Gaetana Agnesi
Mario Andretti
Peter Rodino
Pietro Belluschi
Saint Augustine of Hippo
Saint Francis of Assisi
Vince Lombardi

For more information on these titles and
the Mentoris Project, please visit
www.mentorisproject.org

Made in the USA
Middletown, DE
15 April 2023